THREE
FAMILIES

PEGGY GARDNER

DEDICATION

The families in my novel, *Three Families*, do not bear the slightest resemblance to my large, extended family that is as perfect as one could invent.

So I dedicate this to my children, my brothers, my nieces and nephews, and cousins—and to the memory of my family members who are no longer with us.

A special thanks goes to the Bandon Writers Group, whose support is invaluable.

FOREWARD

One of those nondescript Oklahoma frontier towns, Wolfe Flats straddled the railroad tracks and clung to the rusting shells of cotton gins that were once its great, thumping heart. Wooden cubes of pre-war bungalows lined streets where lava sidewalks buckled. The parched gardens of old women sprouted brave corn and languid squash.

In the first quarter of the century, Wolfe Flats burgeoned. Cotton, corn, and peanuts flourished from the banks of Red River north to the county line. Prosperous and poor farmers, Chickasaws and their former slaves, merchants and horse traders settled down for the long haul.

By the second quarter of the century, Lindberg had crossed the Atlantic, mechanization had disrupted the farm economy, and Wolfe Flats had developed its own social order with Methodists and Baptists vying for the apogee in the community.

Although most of the universe is dark matter, in Wolfe Flats the cows and the people and the stars over their heads are neatly arranged as two quarks, the electron, and the neutrino. Some families, however, defy the order of physics.

One family, the troglodyte Reaves, lived in the West End—Wolfe County's no man's land; a second family, the Poseys, were better off than they should be; and, the third family, the Bulats, in Dubrovnik, unraveled like a broken string of pearls.

If dark matter could give way to light, there is a pattern to be seen in all this as everything and everyone converges toward a single place—a chicken coop of golden Buff Orpingtons where one tortured child hides.

CHAPTER ONE

BUFF ORPINGTONS

Wednesday, July 18, 1981

At exactly three o'clock in the morning, Eliot Posey's prize Buff Orpingtons set up a clamor in the henhouse that would have startled a heavy sleeper. His sister Annabel prided herself on keeping one ear open for the sound of her brother's Commodore, as it hit every pothole from Wolfe Flats to the outskirts of town, where pretentious turrets humped the roof of their Queen Anne house.

Annabel eased the double-barreled shotgun off the gun rack by the back door and tiptoed down the porch steps in her old wool slippers, clutching at the smooth branches of her mother's crepe myrtle for balance.

She aimed the gun high over the henhouse and squeezed the trigger. The burst of gunfire set the Buff Orpingtons into such a cacophony of flapping and cackling that a hungry coyote would surely slink away.

Maybe not. The waning gibbous moon hung so far down in the night sky that Annabel could see small clouds of yellowish feathers wafting out of the henhouse door that was hanging askew.

Annabel leaned the gun against the side of the henhouse, picked up a sizeable club of firewood, and eased the door open with her foot. At forty-eight, some spinsters would be frightened of noises in the night. Not her. Not Annabel Lee Posey.

She thought fondly of her long-dead father, who had named his daughter after Edgar Poe's wispy little heroine. Her father had to settle for a stalwart version of his father-in-law with breasts.

A slanting ray of moonlight lit the interior of the henhouse where beady-eyed hens settled back nervously on their hocks. Except for the fluttering of wings and an occasional squawk, the only sound was an uneasy thumping in her chest, as Annabel stood in the door of the large coop and counted a dozen Buff Orpingtons, twenty-four small, glinting eyes transfixed on her.

And a thirteenth pair of eyes, wide, round, and opaque as the old crown glass in the front door of their Queen Anne.

The creature had disguised herself as a Buff Orpington, her bare toes wrapped around the roosting bar, her thatch of blond hair clinging like dirty feathers to a skull that seemed oversized for her body. Her thin arms doubled up like wings, with her fists rammed into her armpits. Her thin rag of a dress drooped like wet tail feathers.

Annabel silently stuck out her hand; the child took it and swung effortlessly down from her perch, weightless as a newly hatched chick.

They walked hand-in-hand into the flood of a low-hanging moon. The top of the child's head struck Annabel mid-thigh. She might have been five or older. Or younger. Her face flamed in the moonlight like the face of a newborn. Her stork-like legs wobbled, as she crept up the back steps beside Annabel, clutching her hand like a lifeline.

Under the bare bulb dangling overhead by the back door, the child paused, grabbing the edge of her dress to wipe her thighs. The flash of an upstairs light caught her attention.

Not a sound came from her, as a row of perfect, baby-white teeth gleamed under the porch bulb. She twisted her mouth into a grimace and tried to free her hand. Her odd pale eyes gleamed sullenly with the acceptance of betrayal, as though betrayal were an expectation.

"That's my mother's room. She's an old lady. Harmless." Annabel hoped that was the only lie she had to tell this child. Lilymae, her mother, had made harming others a lifetime vocation.

Annabel paused as the girl pulled back, remembering a childhood in which her mother pulled the strings: her father, estranged from Lilymae's bed, his self-esteem nibbled away, until a CVA sent him heavenward; Eliot, her Adonis-like brother, who simply could not spin out the future his mother imagined for him, sputtered around the edges of his life like a snuffed candle after his whore-cum-Raphaelite angel was murdered.

Annabel paused, looking down at a single toe protruding from her wool houseshoes. If her fault-finding mother handed out prizes, she would win the jackpot, a spinster daughter as full of faults as one of Dante's damned, deserving every inch of the small lower circle that had become her life.

She peered down at the child's small, half-open mouth. No loose or missing teeth. She could be as young as four or old as eight. Annabel kept a grip on the child's hand and traced her fingers along the ridge of bony shoulders. She was just a skeleton of a child, malnourished, her face grotesquely puffy from fleabites.

The child stopped struggling and looked up at Annabel with eyes so pale and lifeless that they might have been on a corpse, just waiting for a kind hand to sweep them closed.

A trickle of urine dribbled down the inside of her legs and splattered on Annabel's slippers. The small girl clutched her crotch with both hands and shook as though a fierce wind battered her. Wrenching her hand loose, she dropped down and wrapped her thin arms and legs so tightly around Annabel's leg that her femur and tibia might as well have been encased in plaster.

Annabel stepped along the back hall, stiff-legged, unable to pry the child loose, and opened the door to an enormous bathroom—her father said he built it so field dirt could be "waylaid." He later added three private baths upstairs, but this first-floor bathroom was splendid in size and utility.

A giant, claw-footed tub cupped in and flattened like the back of a swan, making it easy for arthritic bodies to sink and rise effortlessly. Annabel turned on the taps, tested the water, and bent down to plug the drain.

The child released her grip, balanced her chin on the edge of the tub, and stared, mesmerized by something outside her limited experience. Beneath her fine, blond hair, her scalp blossomed with brown rosettes of scabs. Between her bare toes oozed the manure of Buff Orpingtons.

The water was a foot deep and tepid. "We're going to make you feel better by washing some of that chicken pen filth off you," Annabel said, as though the visit to the henhouse prompted the bath. She had never seen a dirtier child. Eliot's well-swept henhouse did not contribute to her filth.

Her pale, blue eyes opened wide; she shook her head slowly and fearfully.

"Here. It's not deep. It's warm." Annabel plunged her hand down in the tub to show the child that the water was safely shallow. She tugged on the rag of the child's dress, lifting it past the protesting arms that had just released her. The child's legs stayed firmly wrapped around Annabel's leg.

"Look!" She kicked off one house slipper, straddled the edge of the tub and plunged her bare foot into the water. "I'm part-way in with you. We'll share."

Annabel lifted the limp-as-a-rag-doll child into the tub and gasped at the sight of her naked body. Purplish bruises tracked along her inner thighs. Puffy stripes crisscrossed her bony back. Red nodules of insect bites trailed around her neck and up both sides of her face.

She clutched Annabel's foot and sat in a frozen posture eying the water waving gently around her.

Annabel picked up a bar of goat milk soap, rubbed it between her hands, and began stroking limbs so thin that she could only feel stick-like bones under the skin. The hair was a challenge. The child shuddered when Annabel splashed water onto her back.

"Prell shampoo. See what a pretty green color it is in the tube? They say it makes your hair *radiantly* clean. Want to try it? You'll have to close your eyes so it doesn't sting."

The child nodded and squinted. Annabel poured a cup of tepid water onto her head and squeezed out a bright green worm of shampoo, massaging it into the child's crusted scalp. Brown foam cascaded down her face. The pale body below flamed. Annabel turned on the sink tap, ran a cup of warm water, poured it over the child's head and pushed a soft towel into her clenched hands.

Lifting her gently out of the murky water, Annabel wrapped her in a bath towel, sat on a nearby chair, and held her until she stopped trembling.

"Do you have a name?" This little waif, this ill-treated changeling, this small, blank-faced child might have alighted in Eliot's henhouse after a long, arduous journey from the nether world and have no name. A wafer of humanity so badly treated might not have been afforded the dignity of a name.

The child was silent, waiting, making no movement under the towel.

"I'll call you Ave. It's a word from the Latin that people use to greet each other." *Or say "goodbye,"* she thought ruefully.

Annabel stood up, still holding the child. "I'm going to take you into the kitchen, get you some milk and a nice bread and butter sandwich. Then, we'll find something for you to wear and get you to bed. It's after three o'clock in the morning."

The child slurped a glass of milk and crammed bread into her mouth with both fists. Other than the noisy eating and drinking, she had not made another sound. Annabel led her upstairs, as the child kept a firm grip on her robe. Opening the door to the spare bedroom next to hers, Annabel flipped on the light.

"Here's a nice bed for you. Lots of covers to keep you warm."

The child glanced fearfully around the room, shook her head, and plastered herself against Annabel, as though she intended to dissolve herself into the flesh of her benefactor.

"You've nothing to fear, Ave. You are safe in this house. Mother is just down the hall. My brother Eliot will be home soon." She wasn't sure about that. When Eliot took off in that Commodore of his, he sometimes didn't come home until noon.

The child clutched her more tightly, so she did the only thing she knew to do. Annabel picked up the child she now thought of as Ave, carried her into her own bedroom, pulled back the covers, laid her gently down and crawled in beside her.

Annabel listened to her scratching the welts on her neck until the Buff Orpington rooster crowed, and they both fell into a deep sleep.

CHAPTER TWO

INTRODUCTIONS

The dull thud of the pendulem in her father's prized longcase clock looped through the silence downstairs. Annabel stared at the child in her bed, her hands folded neatly over her chest as though positioned by an undertaker.

Annabel bent over her, listening for the shallow sounds of breathing, taken aback by the porcelain texture of her skin, waxen in places not inflamed by fleabites. After draping an old undershirt of Eliot's over the end of the bed, she left the child asleep, tip-toed out to the hall, and wrapped her old chenille robe about her as she walked down the stairs and out to the front porch.

Swaths of yellow coneflowers, *Ratibida pinnata*, swayed like a garish chorus line, launching the dog days of summer alongside fields of Big Bluestem and Sideoats Grama,

At the far end of the section line, she could see her brother's car sashaying along the gravel road, swaying back and forth to avoid the potholes. She anticipated his gray, hung-over face, the stench of stale smoke on his clothes. He would have gone no farther than the bars along the state line, on the river. Since Mirna's death, he stayed close to home.

Annabel wanted to tell her brother what she'd found in his chicken house before their mother put her own slant on it. She stepped back into the entry-way, listening to the floor creaking above her, gauging the child's soft-footed movements over to the window and then out to the hall.

Ave descended the stairs, one at a time; her body arched with a theatrical flair, as she stretched her toes tentatively forward. Her watchful expression suggested that each step might lead to a bottomless pit.

Annabel watched Eliot's old t-shirt flapping around her like the rags on Boris Karloff's mummy emerging from a crypt. Near the bottom, the child paused; her eyes darted around the room like a feral animal checking for an escape route before she took the last step.

"Come on down, Ave. Come to me." Annabel held out her hand, the way she would to a strange dog, allowing it time to scent danger or safety, the space to make a decision. Reddish circles puffed along the child's jawline and neck, but the lop-sided swelling on the left side of her face had subsided. Her small hands dragged at her tangled hair, smoothing it behind her ears; she hesitated at the kitchen door.

Annabel watched her mother contemplating Ave from her advantageous chair at the end of a Jacobean table that could seat a dozen. Through the droop of her stroke, Lilymae Posey might be shaping a smile or trying to control the rage she felt over the intrusion of this child.

Ave stared fixedly at her, walked around the table and stood by her chair with her head lowered, as though prepared to accept a blessing or a blow.

The bombshell was delivered in an unexpected way. "She has the Posey chin." Annabel's jaw dropped. "Pointy with a small cleft. Your father had it and his father as well. Eliot favors my mother. I never could decide about you, Annabel."

The back door leading into the kitchen had opened quietly to announce Eliot. The silence of presentiment etiolated Annabel's brother, leaving him pale and blinking in disbelief.

He moved toward the child, as though he'd been caught by a revolving door, fearful to step forward, hesitant, as if an implacable force held him in slow-moving bondage.

The minute the child's ice blue eyes stared up at him, he said only one word: "Mirna."

"I've been calling her Ave. She won't or can't speak. I found her on the roost with your Buff Orpingtons. We need to talk about what else I found. Not in front of the child."

Like an automaton, Ave crawled onto a chair, tucked her feet under her bottom, and grabbed a fistful of bacon with one hand and a biscuit with the other. Shoveling the food into her mouth, she arched her tiny spine, as though waiting for a blow. When it didn't come, she made a second dive for the food.

"Slow down, Ave. You'll make yourself sick. You can eat all you can hold but slowly." Annabel watched her mother's hand snaking forward to move the bacon. She dumped a spoon of scrambled eggs on a plate and smiled in a twisted fashion.

"From Eliot's Buff Orpingtons. You shared their roost. Now, you can share their eggs." She giggled uncomfortably, as though making a joke might be in bad taste under the circumstances. The peal of Ave's laughter rang out, as though she alone appreciated Lilymae's brand of humor.

Eliot followed Annabel into the laundry room, just off the kitchen, and closed the door. The power of speech seemed to have left him. He gulped audibly and formed his words carefully. "You found her where? What do you mean about finding something else?"

For a moment, Annabel was at loss for words. She and Eliot discussed the things that preoccupied rural people: the weather, the crops, tenant issues, their mother's health, and an occasional book—in that order. Abused children had never been a topic.

Annabel responded brusquely. "I found her in your henhouse at around three o'clock this morning. I thought a dog or coyote had broken in. She has large bruises on her thighs and on her pudendum. And what might have been dried semen on her legs. I washed it off."

Her words sounded harsh, clinical. What Annabel wanted to say was exactly how she felt seeing the child standing in the bathtub with muck streaming down her legs. Ragged bruises, the color of dark wine, spread up her emaciated legs and exploded across the tiny, flower-like fold between her legs.

"She's covered in fleabites and welts, as under-nourished as a victim in Dachau, and she had a bump above her eye, as though someone hit her hard. " Annabel paused. "She seems to understand me, but she hasn't spoken a word. I bathed her, fed her, and put her in my bed."

Her next words came unbidden. "She's such a terrified little girl. Wherever she's been for five years, it wasn't under a blue baby blanket by the side of a road."

Annabel regretted her words the moment she uttered them. That year of her brother's manic searches for a phantom baby wrapped in blue and dropped along a country road had exhausted Annabel. Not once had Eliot said: "My child. My lost child," as though searching for a disembodied child made the pain more bearable—as though bagging trash on country roads could change a hopelessly smudged world.

The shift from shock to fury on Eliot's face was metamorphic as he rammed open the door, went to the hall, pulled out a rifle from the gun case and stood with it dangling in helpless hands.

"You'll just frighten her, Eliot. We don't know where she's been or who did this to her, but her feet are bruised. I think she's traveled some distance." Annabel thrust out her hand and plucked the rifle away from her brother. "She might run again if she doesn't trust us."

Like carillon bells chiming in unison, high-pitched and low-pitched giggles came from the kitchen. "If Mother is laughing, the world must have shifted on its axis. Ave stuffs her food in with both hands. I guess she never ate with a runcible spoon," Annabel smiled wryly at her brother.

Within minutes, Eliot returned to the kitchen with an old blue book; the *Book of Nonsense* gleamed in gold relief across its battered cover.

Annabel watched Ave stiffen as Eliot settled into a chair next to her. He flipped the pages and read Edward Lear without looking at the words. His eyes were fixed on the small girl who watched the words and mouthed them silently.

A seemingly endless stream of nursery rhymes and children's poetry followed, as though Eliot knew losing the child's attention would be unbearable. He traced the delicate line of her cheek with his thumb, playing the Pied Piper to an audience of one battered child who eyed him suspiciously, as though she knew all about rat catchers.

CHAPTER THREE

THE POSEY FAMILY

Oklahoma, 1928

Beyond the bungalows and shotgun houses pushed up side by side like cats arching but unable to stretch, four brick colonials, two Tudor revival houses, and one grandiloquent Victorian mansion positioned themselves on the "good" side of the tracks in Wolfe Flats.

A few merchants, two wealthy Chickasaw families, and the banker showed off for the neighbors, who watched them between out-of-date slatted blinds and were keenly aware of their baggage. The Victorian mansion concealed the very private life of the schoolteacher Vernica Roberts, as it had done for her grandmother before her.

To avoid the pitfalls of such neighborly oversight, Edward Posey started construction on a Queen Anne house three miles from Wolfe Flats in 1927, so that his fiancée from Georgia could be settled in a grander manner than she had known.

The second son of a family that tracked its Georgia roots back to the 1750s, Edward Posey was blessed with the profile of Byron and troubled with the same twisted foot that left him with a slightly uneven gait. Unlike Byron, calling himself *le diable boiteux*, the limping devil, Edward played a gimpy game of lawn tennis and trotted debutantes around the dance floor with such an affable air of self-possession that no one dared to look at his feet.

Born in 1903 on a faltering plantation outside of Atlanta, Edward watched his family struggle with depleted soil, in which cotton had reigned as king for more than a century. The migration of sharecroppers to the North and the boll weevil gnawing its way up from Mexico were destabilizing cotton in the South.

As the belles of his childhood looked aslant at the second Posey son—gauging his marital potential with the calculating eyes of generations of women who could add up yield per acre faster than they could crimp a curl—Edward traded his share of the family plantation too cheaply to his older brother. King Cotton offered a different venue for an entrepreneur; Edward headed west to risk his stake on brokering cotton in southwestern states.

Standing in hot fields and pulling bolls apart to check the staple, buying, selling, and gambling on crops in Texas and the Oklahoma bottomlands, Edward prospered. His nights in cheap hotels from Ardmore, Oklahoma, to Lubbock, Texas, convinced him to get off the road as soon as possible.

By the time he nudged elbows with the five percent of Americans who owned one-third of the nation's income, Edward began to dream of permanency. He would find himself a clever and beautiful wife and install her in a house that would rival the antebellum mansions of his native Georgia; he would settle in this new state that was closer to Pisgah than Atlanta.

The gloom of economic inequity in a time when the small farmer was a disappearing breed offered opportunities to Edward; he bought good bottomland along the Red River; he borrowed money and bought more land.

To Edward, it seemed fortuitous when he met his bride-to-be at a boyhood friend's wedding in the summer of 1927 in Atlanta. When he spotted a stunning young woman, trying to fade into a facimile of William Morris wallpaper in a noisy hotel ballroom, it struck him that the socially naïve Lilymae Macabee exceeded his fanciful standard for beauty. She looked exactly like Millais' drowning Ophelia, with her hands helplessly open, while her russet locks streamed over her shoulders; he might have noted the vacuous expression in Lilymae's eyes, but that realization would come much later.

Edward's desire for cleverness in a wife proved difficult to assess in this Methodist preacher's daughter, whose faint air of boredom and diffident manner concealed a third-rate education and a voracious desire to escape her current circumstances.

Until she met Edward Posey, the life of Lilymae was circumscribed by two opposing boundaries: a proselytizing father who had no qualms about sacrificing his daughter on the Methodist altar of his ambitions; and, a shared dark secret tucked so far back that it only surfaced in both of their dreams.

CHAPTER FOUR

THE PREACHER MAN

The Reverend William Macabee was—like Caesar—an ambitious man. By the time that Lilymae was thirteen, her father had gained a sizeable church in Macon.

Motherless at the age of eight and forced to travel for five grueling years with her circuit-riding father, Lilymae pounded uncomplainingly on out-of-tune pianos in brush arbor revivals across half a dozen Georgia counties because a Caesar expects capitulation.

In a carefully staged tableau, the Reverend Macabee would describe the beheading of the virginal Saint Cecilia, who sang to God with her last breath. Then, Lilymae, draped in a white robe, would move like a wraith from behind a makeshift curtain toward the piano.

At the exact moment that her father swooped up cupped arms as though he, himself, cradled the bloody head of a singing saint, Lilymae beat on chipped ivories "Hallelujah! What a Savior" until Satan ran away with his forked tail tucked between his legs.

When darkness fell on the brush arbors and her father loaded the Ford truck with hymnals and stacks of collection plates, Lilymae always played Scarlatti's Sonata in G Minor with a too-heavy left hand. "It's a variation on a hymn," she told her father, who couldn't recognize a hymn without words—or a piano so badly out of tune that Scarlatti might have shuddered to hear such a feast of accidentals.

When her father came home with the news that they were "bound for the promised land"—that he had been assigned to a real church in Macon, Lilymae felt that that the word "promise" might mean a respite from her father's ruthless crusades.

Building denominations were the watchwords at the Georgia Conference that year. The hundreds of new converts gathered into the Methodist fold by the Reverend Macabee could not be ignored, even as his rampant evangelism left a sour taste in the mouths of his fellow preachers.

A church in Macon meant an adjoining parsonage with a tuned piano and a dozen widows bringing casseroles to the preacher and his daughter. It also meant that William Macabee was expected to enroll his daughter in a suitable school and keep his ears open for any suggestion of scandal that might go hand in glove with food-bearing widows and motherless, teenage girls.

William Macabee's ears looked like great, brownish chambered nautiluses attached to his head. After she became engaged to Edward, Lilymae told him that her daddy could "hear" her thoughts, so she avoided thinking as much as she could. That way she could explain away the large gaps in her sense of the world, one that was perfectly in line with Ptolemy's geocentric universe.

William Macabee's attention to his daughter's education had ended when she could read the Bible aloud, quote ten Psalms from memory, and keep a ledger on the takings from every service. Lilymae was almost an artifact of her father's own making, a dutiful daughter—but one whose uncanny resemblance to her dead mother troubled him.

Only one other thing troubled him: the thing that Satan planted in his wife's womb; the thing that pulled the plug on her life's blood; the thing that kept him in fear that Lilymae might remember that terrible night when she was eight years old.

Any other derelictions that had brought him to a pulpit in a prosperous church in Macon gave him as little call for guilt as Jacob pinching his brother's birthright. William Macabee did what he had to do to get to where he needed to go. It was the only talent his daughter inherited from him.

A backwater farmer's son who wheedled his father into selling his small patch of land, William Macabee used the proceeds to slip practically unnoticed into Emory College. With four years of college under his belt and no thought of his destitute father and younger brother, the Reverend Macabee traveled a rural church circuit, secure in the knowledge that God loved the slippery Jacob, who could trick a hairy brother out of his birthright.

Now that his birthright was in hand, William Macabee decided that his image needed a bit of adjusting. As pastor of a sizeable Methodist church in a city, he would be the embodiment of a new apostle, fervent but self-contained, as though God remained in constant communion with him. His daughter, like a handmaiden of old, would reflect the feminine virtues of obedience to her father and absolute reverence for his views.

The administrative board of his church held strong opinions about handmaidens, having none of their own. The daughter of their pastor would attend the Lanier High School for girls on Forsyth Street. Within a week, Lilymae learned how to bob her hair, fashion a Cupid's bow mouth, and apply raspberry rouge.

"A bobbed woman is a disgraced woman," shouted her father when she brought her new and improved self home after a sleepover at a new girlfriend's.

As a compromise, Lilymae took elocution and china painting lessons—and memorized ten more

Psalms by heart. At the same time, she learned the new dance steps, practiced popular tunes when her father was out, and pored over the social pages in the *Atlanta Constitution*. On her mother's side, she had a cousin once removed in Atlanta whose parents sometimes made the small print on those pages. A visit would be in keeping with kinship and Southern hospitality.

CHAPTER FIVE

LILYMAE ACCLIMATIZES

A t the engagement party in October, Atlanta's old guard looked down their collective noses at Lilymae Macabee, as though she were a new form of tropical spiderwort invading their cotton fields.

The swan-necked Lilymae with her copper hair and the smattering of freckles on her nose brought out Edward's protective instincts. Her raspy giggle, her constant fidgeting around strangers, her too-obvious efforts to prove that her musical education went beyond Methodist hymns, with a badly rendered Scarlatti sonata, did not make a good first impression on her fiance's friends and relatives.

The marriageable girls from Edward's set added to Lilymae's discomfort by demonstrating that particular Southern expertise known as veiled rudeness. At the end of the engagement party, tears flooded down her cheeks like the Great Mississippi Flood, as she refused to rejoin the guests.

"I hope you don't think those girls' bad manners represent the way my own family thinks about you—we would never behave that way," Edward said, mopping an excess of eyeliner off his fiancée's cheeks.

She did think that. Lilymae blinked back tears. She knew exactly how Edward's family felt about her—eggshells under their feet every step of the way. In spite of her hurt feelings, she rather admired those wicked girls. They could flay the skin off their victims, layer by layer, smile as they did it, and leave the injured feeling that they somehow deserved exactly what they got. It was a skill she needed to cultivate.

"I think if they got to know me better, they wouldn't be such jealous cats. How would I know where the Macabees come from? My daddy is an important preacher in Macon. I could be a friend to some of those girls. Not a personal friend but a social friend. I can be a very social person," she sniffed against Edward's handkerchief.

"I'm sure you can be very social in the right setting." Edward scanned his friends and relatives clustered like cabals along the foyer. Ancestor worship in Atlanta was the eleventh commandment, and his fiancée was found wanting.

At that moment, Edward pushed his wedding date up to March.

Moving Lilymae to a raw-boned, frontier state like Oklahoma where the mystique of money determined status would allow her to be the "social person" she longed to become—whatever that meant to her.

The Reverend Macabee accepted his daughter's choice of a husband. Posey was a powerful name in the state of Georgia. But, letting her marry in that Popish Episcopal church in Atlanta was not part of the bargain.

When Lilymae led her disgruntled father across the yard and pointed off in the distance to something no one but she and her father could see, he returned a chastened man, almost eager to have the thing done and his daughter on a train to Oklahoma.

"Not to be revealed," Lilymae said when Edward questioned her about how and why her father had changed his mind so abruptly, agreeing to marriage by an Episcopal priest. Lilymae's ashen face caused Edward to swoop her up in his arms. "The macabre is not to be remembered," she whispered—as obtuse as the Delphic oracle. The veil that moved across her eyes hid a fear that Edward had never before seen.

CHAPTER SIX

LILYMAE SETTLES

March 1928

Edward's Queen Anne house in Wolfe County would not qualify as a great architectural statement. Although sprawled out on the prairie, rather than tucked into the hills and dales of England, the house did not appear maladapted. Heavy, dark cedars, dripping with blue berries, formed a protective barrier between the house and the fierce prairie winds that tore down from Kansas.

Additional structures moved higgledy-piggledy behind the house, running around like afterthoughts to an otherwise balanced construct. Barns, sheds, hencoops, and storage bins insisted that rural living be practical.

Practicality did not intrude inside the house. Linen fold paneling of bleached oak buckled handsomely along the entryway. Edward's study boasted tiers of quarter-sawn oak shelving for books; Lilymae's adjoining parlor, with over-sized windows, faced a yet-to-be planted rose garden. Murano glass candelabras wired for the tourist trade hung from every ceiling and cast odd little slivers of light about the rooms, as though they were uneasy so far from their canals.

When Edward brought his bride home from the Wolfe Flats Depot behind a team of gleaming red mules, after a grueling train trip across Georgia, Alabama, Mississippi, and the corner of Arkansas into Oklahoma, she gasped at the sight of the house; for once, she was too startled to speak.

When the nut-brown, squared off body of Hephzibah Kiel moved off the wrap-around porch like a determined tank and clutched her in an affectionate embrace, Lilymae fell into a dead faint.

"I don't amalgamate with the hired help, Edward," Lilymae archly announced to her new husband from the fourposter bed where Hephzibah had left her propped. "We Macabees might not hobnob with society people, but we know where to draw the lines."

Her petulant bottom lip stood out in a way that her husband had first begun to notice on their train trip from Atlanta to Wolfe Flats. He observed other things as well. She snapped at the sleeping car attendant; she made a rude comment about an old woman who was slow getting down the aisle; and, she either stared blankly out the window or thumbed through copies of *McCalls* as she complained of boredom.

Even though he had arranged for a single room car with full toilet facilities and a stationary bed and had booked an adjoining room for privacy, Edward's fantasy of bedding a limp-with-passion, Pre-Raphaelite Ophelia sunk like a stone.

The only description he could muster about his bride was "pliant." Once he worked his way through an old-fashioned corset, yards of a voluminous cotton nightgown, and into a body as malleable as dough, no one appeared to be home.

Lilymae could quote Corinthians to the letter: "For the wife does not have authority over her own body, but the husband does." With marriage came conjugal duty; she didn't have to pretend to participate.

Participation forced itself into her life when her ankles swelled like sausages and her faint freckles darkened into a mask-like Melasma during her first pregnancy. Had it not been for Hephzibah coaxing her down the stairs, plying her with custards, brushing her hair hundreds of strokes a day, and tirelessly anticipating her whims, Lilymae would have remained in bed awaiting the worst.

She knew what might be festering in her belly. "Hide it!" she had hissed to Hephzibah. "If it isn't right, don't let anyone see it."

No baby could have been more "right" than Eliot Posey. Beneath strands of chestnut hair, two dark blue eyes looked curiously up at a mother who held her son stiffly away from her.

"His eyes is the same color as Miz Stewart's bluing. I never seed eyes so purty." Hephzibah filled in an awkward gap, as Edward Posey flinched under the cold stare of a wife who had just endured a hellish delivery.

Lilymae would spend the next year blaming her husband for the torture that he had inflicted on her body. Three months after Eliot's first birthday, the arrival of a Jean Patou ivory china silk dress from Paris and a fur coat styled for the Duchess of Wellington opened Lilymae's bedroom door.

Nine months later, the unstylish Annabel Posey huffed her way effortlessly down the birth canal. In a seemingly loving gesture, her mother caressed her head. She was, in fact, checking for lumps or another tiny face under the bloody mat of nondescript hair.

She handed the baby over to Hephzibah and glared down her acquiline nose at her husband. "A third child would be spitting in the eye of Fate. Won't happen. Don't tempt providence."

Neither providence nor the charms of his wife would tempt Edward Posey again. His character renounced duplicity. He didn't impersonate a

gentleman; he was a gentleman—with gentle manners, compassionate feelings, and the good sense to
know that even if he had not married a lady, he must
make the best of things.

CHAPTER SEVEN

THE BARGAIN

Lilymae Macabee swung like a weighted pendu-
lum from the Macabee family tree over to the
Posey tree after her marriage. Although her father
could preach an off-the-cuff, hell and damnation
sermon that swept his Macon congregation into the
frenzy of repentance, his podium skills carried no
weight in Atlanta where the waltz, the foxtrot, and
the knee-knocking moves of the Charleston captivated young men.

The distant cousin's wedding in Atlanta had
offered Lilymae her first glimpse of a different life.
Her cousin pointed out Edward Posey to her in the
reception line. "There's a catch for you, Lilymae. A
few years ago, he split for Oklahoma where only out-
laws and Indians live. God knows why. All the girls
here are wild about him. Family's real old in these

parts. His mother has blue blood and blue hair. DAR in her veins."

Lilymae missed the train back to Macon, wore out her welcome with her cousin's family, but managed to get herself invited to a soirée where she knew Edward Posey would be. She thumbed through a small book about Schumann, found his courtship of Clara much more interesting than his compositions, and eased into a chair adjoining Edward Posey at the musicale.

In keeping with a man captivated by the placid, self-contained faces of Renaissance Madonnas, Edward Posey was bowled over the second time he saw Lilymae Macabee. She was Fra Filippo Lippi's Salome. *And*, a Salome who knew a great deal about the composer Schumann.

Within two months of letters moving slowly by rail from Macon, Georgia, to Wolfe Flats, Oklahoma, Edward Posey was back on the train, offering the Reverend Macabee a respite from supporting his spinster daughter.

The bargain with his sour-faced father-in-law-to-be included a contribution to the Macon Methodist Church that would *not* be the wedding venue. For generations, the Poseys had married in Atlanta with an Anglican ceremony.

Lilymae's father, two members of his church board, and the Atlanta cousin, once removed, were the only Macabee guests. Had Lilymae realized that Edward's family practiced an odd form of nondiscrimination, she might have sent invitations to her dead mother's poor relations.

She watched the coloreds embracing Edward; an assortment of farmers in ill-fitting suits and people whose names she had seen on the society pages of the *Atlanta Constitution* and the *Atlanta Journal* mingled comfortably under large canopies set up in the Posey orchard. She was appalled to see the social strata lacking definition.

Years later, Lilymae's daughter, Annabel, would look through her mother's scrapbooks at the yellowing pages of Atlanta and Macon newspapers; Lilymae's tight little bridal cap and clenched jaws gave her the appearance of an early-day football player ready to charge the line.

She was ready. Wolfe Flats, Oklahoma, was virgin territory for myth making. There, social history was in its infancy. Only bloodlines of horses and bulls mattered, so Lilymae was free to spin a past that might reel out a fine future.

Self was something to be invented—especially when a person has been handed a lesser self. Deceit and hyperbole were fundamental to the image Lilymae embellished for herself as a Southern belle. If she mentioned her father at all, she misplaced him somewhere in the company of orator preachers like Harry Emerson Fosdick.

In her mind, Lilymae Macabee waxed eloquently about her life. When she edited her past for her children's benefit, they appeared stricken with boredom or collapsed with giggles. So, she went over and over her life in her own head, pleased by her silent philosophizing.

Philosophizing for Lilymae meant imposing fantasies about her husband's youth to become a mélange of the novels of Margaret Mitchell and Taylor Caldwell. She locked away visions of brush arbors and a Janus-faced baby in the shallow grave of her memory.

When Annabel reflected back on her parents, she saw only a chasm of differences between them. Some cosmic force, like Aristotle's linear causality, must have moved them into a temporary alignment until they took full measure of each other and drifted apart.

Annabel's father admired plain, personal honesty. He could afford truth. Her mother could not. The Posey family had recovered their land and capitalized on Yankee greed with multiple commercial enterprises.

"We tholed," her father would say of the Posey family. "Romanced the enemy." Finally, the truisms of the Deep South drove him away—the worn-out cotton fields, Atlanta outgrowing the charm of its past, and hoop-skirted girls decked out for the tourist trade.

The Depression was at hand. It was time to unwind the Posey cocoon. Bottomland near Red

River in Oklahoma could be bought cheaply. The state was raw and new and the journey toward prosperity almost a given for man like Edward Posey with higher hopes for a fine life than the fates would allow.

CHAPTER EIGHT

DANCING

Every life involves a journey of sorts, though most travelers don't have a notion of whether to plod or waltz along that road. Lilymae had made the two-step her preferred mode: two quick and two slow. It came of having a preacher for a father, one who made a habit of ritual humiliation of Lilymae and her mother.

Lilymae learned to jump quickly to stay out of her father's way; she also practiced moving like cold molasses so she wouldn't disturb him. She tried to avoid reflecting back on her childhood, but it intruded into her waking and sleeping hours, the way the rancid odor of a slaughterhouse thickens the air, even after the beasts have disappeared.

She and the Biblical Isaac had a lot in common—waiting for their autocratic fathers to engage in blood letting. William Macabee never struck his wife or daughter, but his censorious tongue was honed. Its sting often came from his pulpit, as he wrapped it around scriptures to humiliate them publicly.

"Your wife will be like a fruitful vine," he assured his parishioners. "The Lord said to be fruitful and multiply." His words spewed as a direct rebuke to his frail wife, Lessie Mae, huddled with their only child in a back pew, trying to be invisible.

The Reverend Macabee considered his near child-less state—with only one scrawny, cinnamon-haired daughter—a test of his faith that would be ameliorated when the Lord saw fit.

During the first four years of marriage, he bore, without complaint, the spotting and cramping that had become second nature to Lessie Mae. When her belly began to swell in a way inconsistent with bloat, he took her to a local midwife who proclaimed her pregnant. He was mildly disappointed with a daughter four months later.

Seven years later as the devil entered the womb of his wife, it did so in a companionable fashion, laying its seed alongside his own every Saturday night as he prayed for a son.

Lilymae crafted her own prayer that God would deliver her mother from the terrible sickness that wracked her body every morning and kept her in bed most of the day. As she wasted into a skeletal thinness, her mother's belly protruded like a diseased burl on a tree.

It was revival week in Dooley County, so Lily-mae's father seized the offer of a free, two-room cabin four miles out of Vye-enna for his wife and daughter.

On that climactic Saturday, after six stirring days of sermons, his feverish wife picked the wrong time to complain about the odd cramps she was having.

William Macabee had his own complaints. "The truck won't start. I'll have to take the horse to get there in time for the meeting. I just hope this storm holds off until I get into town. You stay with your mama, Lilymae. It's too soon for anything to happen with the baby. She had the same kind of cramps with you for weeks before you came," he announced in a crabby tone. "I'll be back just after dark."

Lilymae remembered the purplish sky flashing with streaks of lightning and the odor of sulpher in the air as her father disappeared down the dirt road on the barrel-bodied mare. A rising wind pounded the weather-beaten cabin. A kerosene lamp threw convoluted shadows on the wall.

The furious thunderstorm muffled her mother's screams. Nothing could stem the flow of bright, red blood from between her legs nor the total sense of helplessness that Lilymae knew would never be allowed to visit her mother's eyes again.

The memory of that night was too terrible to sort itself out. Instead of Isaac on that burning altar, it was the thing that came out of her mother. Instead of a white-bearded Abraham, her red-faced, grim father held up a bloody creature with a tiny, lashing tail and a misshapened head.

The storm had passed. The moon was so crystal clear in the night that the shadowy craters on its surface seemed too near. So did the images that would never fade from eight-year-old Lilymae's memory.

In one hand, her father carried that maimed baby by a single bloody foot into the woods; in his other hand was a shovel.

Under the full moon, his daughter thought she could see its head dangling like a medallion with two tiny faces flattened, as on a used coin, watching her with fearful eyes, sending out flashes of desperation.

When her father returned, he said: "Spawn of the Devil. Do not speak of it."

Lilymae didn't speak for six months. Not at her mother's funeral two days later. Not when some of the churchwomen asked about the "miscarriage" and said "you poor thing, you" until she wanted to scream. She found her voice when her father put her in front of an out-of-tune piano and demanded that she "praise the Lord with your God-given talent" in front of strangers.

What Lilymae's youthful voice lacked in timbre, it compensated for in the kind of wracking pain that resonated against notes half a step out of tune:

> "And am I born to die?
> To lay this body down?
> And must my trembling spirit fly
> Into a world unknown."

Her choice of hymns did not bring a successful closure to that particular brush arbor service. It took two more years of practice on a prescribed list of revival hymns before Lilymae could be trusted to support her father's mission.

The night of the "terrible secret" haunted his dreams as well as those of his daughter, but the Reverend Macabee exorcised those dreams by traveling six circuits for the Methodist Episcopal Church. From a mediocre gospel preacher, hardly noticed by the Methodist Conference, he rose to becoming its sometimes-embarrassing star with hundreds of converts.

Later, on the safe cusp of her life as a Posey, Lilymae nattered on about family history, carefully segmenting Edward's family tree into "good" and "bad" branches while leaving the Macabees neglected like noxious weeds edging her new Eden.

Just as a chef reduces a sauce, Lilymae stirred family events round and round in her mind until they thickened into something palatable.

CHAPTER NINE

THE BULAT FAMILY

Croatia, 1974

When Mirna's pious Catholic father doubled his belt and laid it across her back and Jelena's for their terrible discovery, she felt shame, as though the evil he had done as a young man had been passed genetically along, and she and her sister were paying the piper.

Quite by accident, Mirna and Jelena had found the curved-blade knife with an odd wrist strap nestled in a small box lined with red velvet in the back of his closet. They were twins, not identical, but bound so inseparably that either one might speak what the other was thinking.

"Mirna, why would Papa keep such a thing?" Jelena held the knife up by its strap. "It's nasty and caked with something—dark like dried chicken blood."

They had been searching their father's closet while he was at work to see if they could find a few coins on the floor, ones that he wouldn't miss. Sixteen-year-old girls without a lipstick between them could be desperate in those days when Western goods were coming into their city.

Mirna crawled farther back into the closet. Shabby, damp military uniforms hung authoritatively in a row behind her father's stiff woolen suits, as though they anticipated one more use. A large box sat squarely in the far corner of the closet.

When the girls opened it, the world they knew changed. On the front page of a yellowing German newspaper was a photo of their father with a lurid description of what the Ustashe "crusaders" had done to the Serbian inmates at the Jasenovac Camp with a clever tool called the "Serbcutter."

"Drop that nasty thing!" Mirna shouted at her sister. "That's human blood on it."

At the bottom of the box was their father's diary, dating from 1929 when he became an active participant in the Croatian fascist movement through the end of World War II when he went under cover rather than flee the country, as some of his prudent comrades that he called cowards had done.

The girls turned the pages slowly, struggling to grasp the deep pleasures of slashing throats and flicking out eyeballs that their father described as "Dalmatian oysters."

Until that same day when their father came home from work and his daughters confronted him with what they had found in his closet, their home had been a well-ordered place of mourning for four years.

Mirna remembered her father's only show of emotion as he stood over her mother's corpse after her appendix had gone bad. He had wound her long, blond strands of hair around his fingers and lectured her stiffening body for leaving him, all the while sobbing as he spoke.

Across her deathbed, he glanced up coldly and only once at his daughters; they might have been strangers, imposing on something too personal for them to see.

Mirna and Jelena were fraternal twins—yet, their mother insisted that they shared a single placenta in the womb. "You weighed seven pounds, Mirna. Your sister weighed only four. You were looking out after yourself in the womb. Now, you must look after your sister." She meant it as a joke, but Mirna always felt responsible for the fragile Jelena.

The responsibility would be great Mirna knew, listening to the priest chanting *Libera me, Domine* as he sprinkled holy water on their mother's casket.

That day, Mirna watched her father bobbing like a puppet, as church members, who had rarely spoken to him in the past, patted his back and reminded him that his wife was free from pain and heaven bound.

Mirna remembered only Dryden's words on death: "To be we know not what, we know not where." Her mother had gone into darkness leaving only the acrid odor of incense settling over her mourners.

After their mother's funeral, their father became more like himself. Their mother's mantra that he was a loving, hard-working father who wanted the best for his daughters ended with the thump of her coffin lid.

Without their mother's influence, what had been friendly banter turned into barked orders: school reports reviewed weekly; small amounts of money doled out for food; Mass required three times a week; and, prayers offered with clock-like regularity. Their father became militant about polished floors and meals cooked on time, a general in charge of foot soldiers, but he was not a violent man. Not then.

After finding the knife and their father's diary, Mirna recalled that she and Jelena sat like ecclesiastical tribunes waiting for their father that terrible evening—two sixteen-year-olds, tallying up years of hypocrisy, years fecund with self-righteousness.

When he got home that evening, their father eyed them warily. Dinner was not on the table. Jelena shot up from the sofa, holding out the box with the knife, but Mirna spoke first. The first-born should be first to plant her foot in her mouth.

"This knife and these newspapers were in the back of your closet. This is you. Right here." Mirna tapped the yellowed photo of her smiling father, his knife dangling like a phallus from his belt. She feared to mention the diary.

He snatched the box away from Jelena. Mirna watched a curious expression spreading across his face, almost beatific, like the expression Joan of Arc must have worn just before the first tallow-soaked cloth lit her pyre.

"You are grown-up girls now, old enough to appreciate the service I did for the Ustashe. Given enough time, we would have converted the Serbs. There was no time in Jasenovac—too many prisoners, too many fanatics, too many heathens." He stared into space for a moment, vacant eyed, as though he were ordering his thoughts.

"War ended too soon. We had plans with the Bishop . . . but the Russians . . ." his voice trailed off. "The political climate changed. We became ghosts after the War, waiting and hiding, leaving only a credo for our children."

"And the slaughtered bodies of three hundred thousand Serbs, Jews and Roma!" Mirna screamed at her father, unable to look up past a greasy ring around his shirt collar into his eyes.

Their father held the box with the knife before him like a priest with communion wafers, as though daring them to take issue with the visitations made by the sacred blade to dozens of Serbian carotids.

"You didn't know what it was like during the war. Serbs and Jews taking what didn't belong to them. We had to unite against those infidels." He waved his hand across the box the way a priest blesses a pious object. "We offered them a choice—conversion to the true faith or replacement."

The use of her father's word "replacement" struck Mirna as a more evil act of dissembling than his patriotic posturing.

"By *replacement* you mean helping the prisoners exchange this world for the next, Papa? Slicing the throats of unarmed prisoners with that filthy knife?" Mirna shouted. The trace of what might have been a twitch of embarrassment flitted across their father's face; Mirna watched her sister react.

She jerked off her Christopher medal—a gift from their father at their First Communion—and dropped it at his feet. Her words followed like explosives: "You kept souvenirs. Here's another one for you." Jelena sank to the floor, her soft sobs rising and falling like the sound of a trapped creature.

Jelena's medal was a symbol of devotion; Mirna wore hers for decoration. She tossed it on top of Jelena's at her father's feet, watching his face flush violently, as though cardiac arrest might be imminent. Pallor replaced the flush; his lips thinned as he grabbed Jelena by one arm, dragging her up the stairs to his bedroom. Mirna followed. What one twin received, so did the other. *Except the gift of souls when we popped into this world*, thought Mirna. Her soul craved adventure; Jelena's longed for salvation.

They would find neither under their father's roof. He doubled his belt and beat his daughters' backs until blood seeped into their thin cotton blouses. Then, he dropped his belt and tromped out of the house.

When he returned hours later, they could hear the creak of the stairs and the sound of his voice quoting Proverbs. "Do not withhold discipline from a child; if you strike him with a rod, he will not die. If you strike him with the rod, you will save his soul from Sheol."

After that shocking evening, a kind of stilted civility replaced the tension in the Bulat house. A new set of rules was imposed. The girls would attend their Catholic school as usual, but Mirna could no longer take English lessons from Sister Marta because "she was getting Western ideas." They could not leave the house or have their friends over. The radio was locked in their father's room. He cut them off from the wider world.

Mirna remembered the sense of shame she felt at school. She and Jelena knew their friends talked about them, wondering what they had done to deserve prison.

A new girl, Juta, whose frowsy perm and shaven legs marked her as fast, became Mirna's new, best friend. When Juta pranced into the classroom half-way through the term, with her gray regulation skirt hiked to an indecent level, Sister Marta had snatched a handkerchief from somewhere inside her vast gray woolen habit and wiped it, wordlessly, across Juta's red slash of a mouth. Juta eased into the desk next to Mirna's and winked. The floodgates of friendship opened.

Juta sat by Mirna at lunch every day, talking nonstop about her family. "My Ma was a Roma, a gypsy. She's dead. Suffocated by Catholicism." She glared across the room at a cluster of nuns.

"Papa makes me go to this school. He married a woman from Dubrovnik. That's why we moved here. He listens to everything that bitch says against me. I despise her. I do like my brother Milo. He's just a stepbrother by marriage, older, works on the tankers, gone most of the time. My stepmother is a slut."

Mirna punched Juta in the ribs. Sister Marta was heading their way, weaving around the crowded tables of lunches that smelled oppressively of cabbage.

"Grinds the butcher, the baker, the candlestick maker every time she has a chance." Juta whispered just loud enough for everyone around to hear. She beamed up at Sister Marta. "Hello, Sister. I was just quoting an old nursery rhyme for Mirna and Jelena. We just never outgrow our love for poems we heard as children."

She was that kind of girl—eager to shock, walking a fine line, hoping the nuns would throw her out of school. She told Mirna something else the next day, something that planted an idea Mirna wouldn't have time to regret.

"Milo got into port last night and stopped by for a visit. He told me a secret." She looked around to be sure that no one was listening this time. "Milo has ways to help girls get to America. He says lots of jobs are available for pretty girls, as secretaries and such. If they speak some English, he can get visas and hide them on a tanker until they dock in some Mexican port and then go across the border."

Juta's smug face hid other secrets; her stepbrother gave her money for introducing him to girls who wanted a better life, a life in America where every day was an Easter parade of fashion, and movie stars lived just down the street.

Before their father locked them away from life, Mirna and Jelena had seen the black and white movies. They had watched Fred Astaire's tapping feet and longed to sway in a rich man's arms like the willowy Ginger Rogers.

Two weeks later, on a Sunday in April, when the sky hung with gray sheets of clouds above the harbor in Dubrovnik, Mirna and Jelena and crept behind Milo, as he hunched alongside a great, rusty tanker at the far end of the harbor. Dark birds circled above.

Chains from a tall crane positioned over a stack of wooden crates clanged in the brisk sea breeze. Mirna thought about a poem of Shelley that Sister Marta made her memorize and froze.

"The death knell is ringing
The raven is singing
The earthworm is creeping
The mourners are weeping
Ding dong, bell . . ."

The hand that gripped her shoulder should have cemented the foreboding feeling she was experiencing. Milo's oily, slicked-down hair gave him the air of one of those gangsters in old black and white movies.

The thin slits of his eyes glittered in spite of an overcast sky. "Pay attention, Mirna! Don't dawdle. Be sure no one is watching when you and Jelena get into the crate, third one to the right by the gangplank. You'll find a blanket and water inside."

"After we get underway, I'll come after dark to take you to a place below where you and the girls will stay. They'll be six of you on this trip. No talking. No noise. You do everything I say from now on."

Mirna instinctively stepped back, pulling away from the grip that was pushing her toward a huge crate marked with numbers and symbols that appeared cabalistic.

Milo loosened his grip and smiled, if a sneer can resemble a smile. "You girls are friends of Juta's. I promised her only good things will come your way. You just trust me."

An old sepia sketch of Saint George slaying the dragon by Rubens in one of Sister Marta's art books came to Mirna's mind. Milo's face looked exactly like that of Saint George—composed, tranquil, almost bored as he plunges his spear into the dragon's heart. At that moment, she knew she should have grabbed the hand of her sister and run back to face her father's wrath.

When Jelena came back to her pallet the second night at sea, the sight of her bloody thighs sickened Mirna; the vacant eyes and silly smile that refused to go away terrified her. She clutched Jelena against her, as the cold metal tomb they rode in thumped and groaned across the ocean.

She remembered the moment when their father took them to his bedroom, pointed to the high, four-poster bed and slowly snaked his belt from the loops of his thick woolen trousers. She hadn't flinched beneath those blows; she had forced herself not to move, to offer her soft flesh as atonement for her father's sins.

There would be no atonement for the sin against Jelena. Evil had moved as thick as treacle into their lives. Milo's sheepish grin as he dragged Jelena out of their cubbyhole "for a little visit to the captain" should have sent Mirna screaming through the maze of the old tanker to find her sister.

Now, Jelena was lost forever. The wounded girl who returned to a filthy pile of blankets below deck didn't seem to recognize Mirna. When Mirna lifted the pale strands of hair away from Jelena's forehead, a large red nodule bulged just above her delicate right eyebrow.

Jelena shoved aside Mirna's hand, dropped to the pile of filthy blankets, pulled one over her head and began swatting the space around her and muttering, "Get thee behind me" over and over.

"She's unhinged. No one is anywhere near her," a sharp-featured girl named Nadia hissed.

"Satan is," Mirna said quietly as she sank down by her sister and wrapped her arms around an inert clump of blankets.

Satan stayed aboard for the next eight days as all of the girls but Mirna visited the captain. Milo forced her to walk on the deck with him after dark. "You'll get sick staying down in that hole without any exercise. You're the prize of that lot, Mirna." He hugged her against him. "Legs up to here and good English. I'm saving you for something better. Maybe me."

"Chetnik!" The word she snarled startled her almost as much as it did Milo. Without a sound, he twisted the arm he was holding behind her back up and up until she could feel her ligaments screaming. For one instant, she coveted that bloody knife of her father's.

"When I say 'maybe me' you ungrateful Catholic bitch, get down on your knees and thank me." He shoved her face down on the cold metal deck. "That crazy sister of yours is a liability." He leered down at her. "The captain told me she made the sign of the cross so many times that he had to crack her across the head. The girls tell me she's a psycho. I could save myself a headache by throwing her overboard."

Mirna pushed herself up, clutching her aching shoulder, and stared unflinchingly at Milo. "She won't be any trouble. I'll take care of her. I will do anything you say if you leave Jelena alone." Mirna looked into a Stygian ocean, marked only by hopeful splashes of white caps. "You throw her over, I will join her."

Nadia, who bore an uncanny resemblance to a fox with her dark, curious eyes and ruff of sandy hair, spoke in a matter-of-fact manner to Mirna as she ran her hands along a heavily perspiring Jelena two days following her visit to the captain. "Elevated heartbeat and fast respiration. I've seen patients with blood poisoning have these symptoms."

Mirna pushed Nadia away from her sister. "She just needs to eat and drink more water. You're not a doctor."

"Medical aide—second and third shifts since I was fourteen years old. I know what I know. Your sister won't make it without antibiotics. I'll get Milo to find out what this ship has in its medicine cabinet. He owes your sister."

Nadia returned with two out-of-date bottles of tetracycline and a split lip. "Bastard popped me one when I asked for the ship's doctor to see Jelena.

Milo says only the captain and two crew members know we're on board. They don't have a real doctor, just someone who can put in stitches and splint broken bones."

She handed Mirna the tetracycline. "I convinced Milo that Jelena wouldn't make it without antibiotics, so he pried the lock off the medicine cabinet. It's three years past use date but it might help."

Although she had made the threat, Mirna did not join her sister—stiffened and bound by hemp rope into a dirty blanket—as Jelena slipped noiselessly into the vastness of the sea a few miles from Veracruz. She might have, but Milo hobbled her with a chain around her ankles.

"I'm doing you a kindness to let you have your little ceremony." Four girls, none of them religious, made swooping signs of the cross into the setting sun as Mirna stood dry-eyed by the sixth girl in a coffin-shaped package with weights.

Eugene Bulat would have chanted the Joyful Mysteries, the Luminous Mysteries, the Sorrowful Mysteries, and the Glorious Mysteries over the corpse of his daughter without daring to ask God why her young heart had to fail in terror and pain.

Mirna pressed one hand against the bundle where she thought her sister's stilled heart rested and was strangely comforted by Byron:

"If I should meet thee
After long years
How should I greet thee?
With silence and tears."

CHAPTER TEN

THE REAVE FAMILY

Indian Territory, 1905

For slack-jawed, bandy-legged Abner Reave, Indian Territory held the promise of an interrupted sexual encounter: fecund, lush, and unfinished. Like the musk of a rutting dog, this nympholeptic patriarch gave off the scent of opportunity that cemented the loyalty of the ragtag clan that followed him from East Texas by wagon and on foot.

The map of Indian Territory showing the Red River looping like a hangman's noose between Texas and the Territory was as prophetic as the Book of Revelations for a man like Abner with second sight.

Getting out of Texas before their neighbors' accusations of polygamy came home to roost was the first order of business; the second order would be to find cheap land in a territory squabbling over land patents, the Enabling Act, and Indian rights before statehood squelched opportunity.

When Abner Reave stood with thirty of his blood kin on Texas soil above Worthington's Ferry, looking across the Red River into Indian Territory, he was seized by an inchoate longing. Avarice was his soul mate. This was something else. Something that denied naming, almost like desire.

Abner glanced over at the women in his clan, their arms and legs scrawny from the long march on nothing but weevily hardtack; lank strands of non-descript brown hair topped their squared-off faces; their uniformly muddy eyes lacked wishfulness. Two of his three wives were serviceable; the third, Becky, had refuted him. Watching this roiling river furrowing the bank, Abner dreamed of desire again.

On this crisp fall morning, the thick stands of willow along the river swung their yellowing branches, like young girls drying their hair in the afternoon sun. Abner had seen those girls prancing along the town streets, tossing their bright hair, their pink cheeks flaming, their blue eyes putting the sky to shame.

The Reave clan—men, women and children— came in one hue: a relentless brown. Babies might pop out with a hint of buff, like well-chewed leather. By the time they walked on small, bandy legs, their skin, their eyes, and their hair marked them as Reaves.

His family needed new blood—just like his cows needed a different bull—but outside blood was hard to come by. He looked over at his only son, Admah, a greedy boy clamped onto his mother's nipple. Two bright, caramel-colored eyes stared knowingly into his. Becky, his third wife, was a distant cousin. This new son of his might change the cycle.

Abner's hobnailed heel smashed into a clump of daisies tucked into the riverbank. When the fall rains began, the Red River would bring a greasy swirl of currents spreading over the bottomlands, like a gauzy bandage, dark as dried blood and fertile as the Nile.

Abner scowled at the men working the ferry who were pretending not to be staring. The Reaves always elicited curious, faintly embarrassed glances. Their knobby wrists hung below a thin band of dirty cotton known as a "dress shirt" they had put on special for this occasion. They didn't belong here where the River spawned new life. The Wolfe family, half-breed Chickasaws, rich as lords, owned much of this land.

Determined as a colony of purposeful ants, the Reave clan would cross the River, head toward the cheap, arid land eight miles north and west, submerge themselves into half-buried dugouts, and hope to get a turnip crop in before winter.

"Becky!" Abner gestured toward his son's mother. With the birth of her first child a year ago, Becky's ill nature surfaced. Childbirth upset the scheme of things with him and Becky. She now denied him her bed. She refused a third wife's humble position in his household.

He could not discipline his own son. He could no longer smack Becky up beside her head to remove her resentful expression, as he had in the past. She had made him agree to a screwball notion: when they finally settled in the Territory, their son Admah would go to a real school.

A vacuous, half-smile replaced the habitual frown of resentment on Becky's face as she eased forward from the group of women. When her long skirt covered her chicken-thin legs, she didn't look half bad. She was good at winkling out promises and an expert at wheedling.

"Git down there and make them fellers an offer. They's askin' fifty cents for a wagon and ten cents for each of us. Coax 'em down. Inveigle them." Abner liked to use words that would create a flash of blankness in Becky's eyes. Gave him the upper hand. "We cain't spend that kind of money to cross."

Squat and hunched along the riverbank, the tips of their fingers brushing their knees, the men in the clan peered out at a hostile world through identical sets of brown eyes set beneath heavy brow ridges. Their eyes were canny, sizing up the men standing next to the posts on the bank who were trying not to stare as they adjusted ropes on the ferry.

With a signal from Becky's hand, the Reaves cascaded down the bank with a team of mules, two wagons, six cows, and ten pigs. When the bargain was struck, women and children and Abner stood silent as statues on the turbid river, like a family that might have floated down the Auvergne 130,000 years ago.

Once safe on the Territory side, Abner shouted back to the men of his clan: "Wagons and one man to hep load the pigs. The rest of yorn push them cows acrost with the mules a quarter mile downstream. Becky made the bargain. Ast her. Blame her, not me."

He twisted his mouth into the semblance of a grin as he watched his brothers and cousins and nephews looking fearfully at the river. *If it washed a couple of them away, food might not be such an issue for the upcoming winter on new land with no crops. They'd better not lose them mules or cows.*

It would take more than a quicksand-studded river to eliminate members of the Reave clan. They confirmed Mr. Warden's 1936 thesis when he wrote that humanoid stock "must become specialized along human lines or forever perish from the earth." Those parallel helices traveling along generation after generation had betrayed the Reaves with their throwback brows and heavy jaws but rewarded them with tenacity for life.

As the leader, Abner Reave was the shrewdest member of this band of humanoids. No primate could size up an opportunity faster than Abner. In losing his prehensile tail, he had gained a prehensile spirit. Grasping was his way of life. Coaxing was his métier.

From his Sunday pulpit, he could fire up beddable cousins and harden the breast buds on their girl children with the furor of an apostle. Like Solomon, Abner held the land and the sexual energy of his clan—except for that lost sheep Becky, his third wife.

The clan bred, interbred, and produced a high number of stillborn babies; their children sickened and died having experienced only Abner's Sunday sermons and molasses candy as a treat.

Not Admah. As Abner's only son, Admah was special. Abner had not had a good run of breeding—six girls from two wives who showed respect and only one son from Becky who hated the sight of him.

Abner knew the family needed new blood. Any animal breeder knows you need a neighbor's bull to jump the fence to keep cattle from producing sickly, underweight calves. It had been up to Abner to jump that fence.

The "fence" was a distant cousin down by Midland with a sixteen-year-old daughter who could read and do figures. She cut her hair and sang "Under the Bamboo Tree" to spite her daddy, who craved peace in his household.

For an Old Testament believer, polygamy wasn't a sin. A sassy daughter was. Negotiations with the distant relative took place before Abner's clan got wind of his plans. Both of his wives sent out a perpetual flood of sullen sighs during Abner's sermon about his divine sign: "Just as I am, Isaac was forty years old when God sent him Rebecca."

Any other woman would have been bowled over by Abner's marriage oration, right out of Proverbs, proclaiming that a virtuous woman's price is far above rubies, as he placed a cheap circle of 10-caret gold on her finger.

Becky's price was a brace of good red mules. It took two mule straps to tie her to the marriage bed that first night and every night for the next three weeks, until Abner tired of the struggle and went back to the beds of his compliant wives.

His other wives despised Becky, hated her uppity ways, and made her life as miserable as possible. Abner did not intervene. She was a testy, ungrateful misfit in the clan. He regretted the loss of his good mules.

Three months later, Becky's belly began to swell above those thin legs, and the hatred in her yellowish eyes glinted like a trapped cat. Six months later, on a camp cot in a cold lean-to, with the clan's midwife screeching at her to push, Becky Reave expelled a boy.

When Abner got the news that he had a son, he rushed into a lean-to that held the metallic stench of fresh blood. The baby had been carefully cleaned and wrapped. Becky lay on a dirty, bloodstained flour sack with an oozing placenta clamped between her thighs.

Her eyes pinned him with a contemptuous stare. She lifted the child, pulled the blanket aside, and cradled his tiny penis and ecru-colored scrotum in her hand.

"Time to bargain, Abner. Your first. My last." Her flat-featured, ashen face with the crude headboard behind it resembled a 13th Century Madonna, having seen and come to terms with the future.

She fondled the small neck of the baby that squirmed beneath her rawboned hand. "Babies are flimsy. New mamas can be clumsy. Considering your record, this might be your only son."

Abner stepped forward and stopped in his tracks as she held his son up with one shaking arm—too high up, over the hard-packed dirt floor.

"New rules. My rules. You never lay your filthy hands on me again—not on my private parts, not on my body anywhere. You never hit this boy."

Abner gaped at her as though an alien had invaded his clan. His mouth began to work silently.

"Don't say it. Don't you dare. No spare the rod, spoil the child shit. Save it for a sermon. You can tell them two wives of yours I ain't their slave. I had me a boy. I do my fair share. Nothing more."

Becky rubbed a thumb across the baby's brow. "He's a Reave. My daddy claimed this is the mark of Ham—but with space for a big brain behind it. You can teach him how to work. He goes to school when it's time. Not that church school of yours. A real one."

She groaned, drew her legs up and kicked a slimy, gelatinous mass out of the bed where it landed next to Abner's feet. "Bury it so the coyotes don't eat it. I said my say. Send my cousin Clydene in with soap and something good to eat. I'm tired." With that, Becky stretched out her legs, tucked her baby under her arm, clenched her mouth into something resembling a smile, and fell asleep.

CHAPTER ELEVEN

PEANUT LAND

With no bottomland available and the dream of cotton vaporized by drought, the Reave clan moved north and west of the Red River where an occasional windmill clanged above monotonous, flat land. The landscape here struck a familiar note with the Reaves. Kiowas and Comanches starved on it, but they were hunters, not gatherers. The Reaves could collect a neighbor's hogs, eggs from under his setting hens, and corn just before the raccoons got it.

Abner traded the last of their cash, four kegs of rotgut whiskey, four mules and one cow with cancer eye for a half section of barren land in the West End; by happenstance, he discovered legume heaven. Peanut land. Three hundred and twenty acres of well-drained, sandy soil. Boiled peanuts became a staple of the Reaves' diet. Fiber and oil from peanut shells fattened their hogs.

With Abner controlling the purse strings, the clan had limited access to frontier cultural institutions like banks and grocery stores and a school that sprang up in Wolfe Flats when the railroad cut through the middle of the Territory.

With the Four Horsemen always at his back, Abner secluded his clan. Their lean-tos, as graceless and primitive as when they first settled on the land, marked the boundary from the squared off homestead houses of their West End neighbors.

Years later, when the REA came along the south boundary, hoisting tree trunks to be linked by arms of electric wires, Abner preached against pestilence, as though the bubonic plague and an electric current were companions in the spread of disease.

Abner protected his flock against flush toilets, radios, and Baptist churches. Before a barn was raised to protect the winter hay and livestock, the Reaves built their church, hacked the altar cross from a diseased elm, and positioned backless benches for thirty adults and numerous children.

The church accommodated funerals, weddings, and Abner's take on the Scriptures; and, it served as the only school for Reave children. They learned to read from the Bible. They learned that the sun rotated around the earth. They learned that all creatures hung in order of their "humanness" from a golden chain, with the angels at the top. They learned that they were like the Old Testament tribes and destined to wander as a family. They learned that Abner's word—loosely based on God's word—was the law. They learned to be silent around their neighbors, around Others.

Crops had to be taken to town and traded for flour, sugar, and kerosene. On the streets of Wolfe Flats, they watched the Others talking to strangers, crossing prairies and rivers to marry them. Kin meant nothing to the Others. Abner said God's wrath would descend on them for their ungodliness.

Yet, they appeared to prosper in the face of God's displeasure. Sometimes their children were golden in the sunlight. Usually, their bodies were straight.

Abner's Israelites, the chosen people, seethed with unexpressed despair when too many of their babies popped out stunted in body and mind and when deals for choice bottomland took place behind doors closed to them.

Doors might not be closed to Admah, Abner's boy by his distant cousin Becky. Admah sported the clan's distinctive, deep-set eyes, though his had a yellowish cast. Like other males in the clan, his barrel chest vaulted forward; his hands swung almost to his knees. But his legs were long and straight, his teeth squared off and white in a mouth like his mother's with the same power to fiddle with Abner.

When the clan settled in the West End, Becky moved into her own lean-to on the far edge of the compound. Abner parked his boots under the beds of his first two wives and preached from Ephesians: "Wives submit to your husbands as to the Lord."

When Abner stopped by Becky's lean-to to visit his son, his boots never left his feet.

On Admah's eighth birthday, Abner bought him a fat paint pony and preached the next Sunday from Proverbs: "Wisdom is supreme; therefore, get wisdom."

Though the word was not in their lexicon, Abner's clan understood dissembling. When Admah's pony trotted off to Wolfe Flats the following Monday morning, they muttered about promises to no-account wives and children getting above themselves.

Until he was fourteen, Admah missed no more than half of every school year, becoming a good reader and competent with figures. Scorned by the other children at first, Admah developed a position of power in the back of the classroom where the oversized boys sat—leverage through intimidation was only used when necessary.

In public places, servility served as camouflage for the clan. Admah opted for stupidity and reserved a doltish expression for his teacher to escape unwanted attention.

When Abner needed his son in the fields, work took precedence. Becky had no quarrel with that. Harvests and well-tended animals meant food in the larder for winter and shoes for Admah.

Becky prided herself on sacrificing for her son. Her mismatched feed sack dresses testified to her acceptance of whatever odd colors and patterns the other Reave women discarded. She knew that a quagmire of acrimony among the women might be set off by the slightest infraction of their unspoken rules. Resentment and jealousy festered in such a tightly knit community.

At times, the schooling of Becky's son was a bone of contention, but Admah understood clan ethics: hubris is a sin against the body politic. With downcast eyes and slumped shoulders, Becky's boy affirmed his relatives' suspicion of public education as "nothin' worth talkin' about." A boy with a photographic memory needed to keep his own secrets.

Under the flicker of a kerosene lamp at night in the smallest lean-to in the compound, Admah showed his mother his schoolbooks. He described with total accuracy everything he had heard and seen at school every day.

When Becky glimpsed herself in the wavering mirror above the washbasin, she saw only a vague facsimile of the girl who had gone unwillingly to Abner's bed. A face brown as a nut stared back at her. Wrinkles ploughed deep grooves around her mouth; her face looked more like her grandmother's than her own. Her dull, brown hair, threaded with gray, hung in uneven braids. The mirror reflected a woman sapped and spent before her time, a woman to be pitied by other women.

The mirror failed to catch the fire in a pair of hazel eyes that gleamed with inexpressible satisfaction.

Humbling herself before the women of the clan had been no sacrifice compared to all that learning her clever boy brought home.

When Admah was fourteen, he brought home something else: The Great Pandemic. Influenza raced through the clan faster than the Mongols smashed into Bukhar. With weakened immune systems because of rare outside contacts, members of almost every family fell under attack to fatigue, violent coughing, and, finally, the high fever that no amount of pond water or Abner's praying could lessen.

Abner's first wife sponged off a stiff, yellowed Becky and sewed her into her second-best quilt so that her son would remember colors bright as a child's puzzle and not his mother going into the sandy soil. Coffins were a luxury in the best of times. A fourteen-year-old boy who looked like a man but wept like a child would not notice a shroud replacing a box.

CHAPTER TWELVE

ADMAH'S RESISTANCE

After his mother's death, Admah drifted back into the clan's way of life, traveling into Wolfe Flats to help his father haul peanuts or to take corn to be ground at the mill. The cycle of planting and harvesting and praying for more rain or less rain imposed the kind of monotonous rhythm that Admah craved in order to forget a mother who had so eagerly waited for him at the end of the day.

Admah attended his father's church. He abided by the clan's rules—except for praying. When God abandoned his mother, Admah gave up on God. Admah's lips moved in church; the dedication on his face would put an apostle to shame.

Even if a clan member could hear his words, they would assume he was speaking in tongues. "Jabberwocky" recited under his breath and backward sent "slithy toves" up to heaven as fast as Admah could dispatch them.

The news that bombs had dropped on Pearl Harbor and their nation was girding itself for war had no effect on the clan. Unlike the brazen South firing on Fort Sumter, the Reaves seceded without a whisper to mark their defection.

Admah hunkered down in the West End with his cousins, far from those fierce blue-ink posters of Uncle Sam with a pointing finger that marked them as cowards. Abner preached: "We line up with the conscientious objectors. We retreat from the sin of killing. We deplore the spilling of American blood on foreign soil."

Abner did not deplore the increased price for his crops. In the War years, every man, woman, and child worked from sunup to sundown during growing and harvesting seasons. Abner and one male—too old for the draft—took produce into Wolfe Flats to trade for whatever wasn't rationed.

No Reave would dare apply for a ration book. The government wanted particulars. Names, family members, ages. That was dangerous information for invisible people. The Government liked having Philistines, Babylonians, and Canaanites all under one roof. Chosen people didn't have a prayer if they let the Government know where they lived.

The clan didn't need anything the Government had to offer. They governed themselves. An individual who hoarded eggs when the chickens didn't lay or stored bricks of butter down in a cistern committed crimes against the unspoken socialist philosophy of the greater Reave family.

However, the "natural" weaknesses in men's nature such as bedding another man's wife or taking a girl child by force could be remedied by the trade of a cow for an insult or a quick marriage to right the wrong.

Abner could legislate almost any wrong to the community's satisfaction. If he couldn't, he chewed the fat with God. God would understand why a man of Abner's standing kept a hoard of black market sugar while the rest of his people managed on molasses for their sweetening,

At the end of the War, the taste of sugar wafted into clan territory. When Abner's son, Admah, no longer feared conscription, he drove a load of peanuts into Wolfe Flats and came home with a battery-powered radio. "We need weather reports, Pa. It's good business to hear the farm report."

"When I take my sugar to tea," blasting out of Becky's lean-to, that Admah now claimed for his own, set Abner's teeth on edge. Popular music corrupted young people. Watching Admah in the fields—sweat pouring off his cantaloupe humps of shoulders and his leg muscles working like a mule's—put a traveling notion into Abner's head.

Admah showed no interest in any of the marriageable girls in the clan; as soon as the harvest was over, Abner took his son to the Wolfe Flats Depot and bought train tickets to Lubbock, Texas. "It's time to meet other folk like ourn. Second and third cousins, once removed."

A distant cousin with better teeth than most of their other cousins brought half a dozen teenage girls to meet Admah at a community church service in Lubbock. Out of courtesy, the elder asked Abner to give the sermon.

To a room full of dowdy girls and women, wearing nothing more flamboyant than a floral headscarf to spite the East Texas winds, Abner preached a favorite sermon: "The rock of our church, Saint Peter, speaks against outward adornment, against hair braided too fancy, against jewels and fine clothes."

As if the sermon wasn't depressing enough, an air of desperation hung over the community room of the church where mothers had lined up mile-high cakes and lard-crusted pies to tempt a potential son-in-law. That strapping young man who looked somewhat like every other man of their acquaintance ignored their daughters, as Abner pushed him from family group to family group.

On the train trip back to Wolfe Flats, Abner catalogued the genealogy of the families, ending with his choice. "Pearly Talbut, daughter of my third cousin,

Winnie Reave before she married one of them Talbuts down by Odessa. I thought for pure dee shapeliness, she had them other gals beat by a mile." He smiled over at his noncommittal son. "A fellow likes a substantial posterior on his woman. I could tell you . . ."

"Don't! It's steatopygia!" The abruptness of Admah's retort startled his father. "It runs in our family," Admah added.

Abner turned a slack jaw toward his son, as though he had just announced a communicable disease.

"Fatty deposits. Genetic. I read about it in a *National Geographic*. Sometimes, I brought them home for Ma to read. Our teacher left old ones for us to take. Ma said you never let her have anything but the Bible to read. We disobeyed you and hid them." He glared at his father.

"I'm getting ready to disobey you again, Pa. No cousins. I don't find them interesting. They smell like lye soap. I pick my own wife. I've been thinking about someone." He refused to say more and plastered his face against the train window, committing every detail of the landscape to memory, in case he never took another trip.

When they returned to the West End, Abner's next sermon was from Proverbs: "A wife of noble character is her husband's crown, but a disgraceful wife is like decay in his bones."

Admah did not stay to listen. He was on his way to Wolfe Flats to find a girl who did not smell of lye soap.

CHAPTER THIRTEEN

FIRST BRIDE

The scent of rosewater and the sound of music wafted about Essie Holt. When Admah heard Dick Haynes sing: "The moon was all aglow and heaven was in your eyes" on the Victrola in Essie's living room, he experienced a bolt of lust that kept his horse in a continual lather with trips into Wolfe Flats until Essie agreed to a secret marriage in the Reave Community Church.

Admah broke the clan code by choosing one of the Others as his lawfully wedded wife. Too tall for a woman, with a backside flat as a board fence, Essie posed no threat to the other Reave women. They pitied her ignorance, her clumsiness, and her long, bloody, unproductive births.

Her father-in-law pronounced doom when Admah arrived late one evening with a town girl in tow. "Readers make poor breeders." Secretly, Abner was pleased that his son had whisked away one of those town girls. By jumping the fence, he had brought new blood into the clan.

Of more importance, his son set Wolfe Flats on its ear, made its men folk uneasy about their women—about bulls that leave their herds. Before his son brought Essie home, Abner considered his dealings with merchants a self-inflicted kick in the teeth—those sideways glances, the faint snickers when they thought his back was turned, and the under weighing of his yields.

After the marriage, Abner didn't care that his new daughter-in-law's father, who owned Holt's Dry Goods, cut his daughter when she rode into town with Admah and that Essie wept until no more tears would come.

A woman who couldn't wring the neck of a chicken was a sorry piece of goods. Still, Abner considered his daughter-in-law a bargain for three reasons: she bred quickly; she could teach the clan's children; and, her hair was the color of corn silk.

Ten years later, with seven, stillborn babies lining the edge of a fencerow behind the church, the merchant's daughter had saddled Abner's son with more woes than Job. That was Abner's opinion, and he prayed on it until it became a fact with a solution. Getting Admah to accept the solution proved tricky.

"It's like this, son," Abner flung his bony arm around his boy's shoulder. "Without you, our line ends. That's a sorrowful thing to me. My wives done quit their bleeding." He stared hopefully into a face that gazed back in stony silence.

"They's nothin' I wanted more than to see little tow heads, maybe with blue eyes, pop out of Essie. Her womb won't carry a child to term. You wouldn't keep a cow like that in a herd. She'd have to go."

Admah yanked away from his father's arm. "You misunderstand me, boy. I was givin' you an analogy. Like the Scriptures give us practical examples to understand higher things. I have a fondness for Essie. She's not a complaining woman. She tries hard. She'd always have the place of honor in your house and be cared for by your new wife."

"Essie is a good wife. She don't refuse me," Admah gave his father a sly look, remembering that his own mother had cast Abner out of her bed. "That's why she's five months gone with this next one—longer than t'others. I promised not to tell. Bad luck, she says, to think of them stones out there."

Essie could think of nothing else, though she purposefully avoided visiting the run-down family cemetery where most markers were simple boards with names gouged into them or a hump of sandstone with no identifying mark beyond a family memory.

Painstakingly, Essie had carved seven dates and seven names onto the smoothest slabs of sandstone she could find: Aaron, Benjamin, Caleb, Daniel, Eli, Felix, and Gideon.

Refusing to keep a manly distance, Admah hovered outside the lean-to where Essie writhed in absolute silence, as the family's midwife shoved on her swollen belly to turn a child determined to back itself into this world.

No man would enter a birthing place until the mess was cleaned up. It would be off-putting. Admah stood outside the door, shuffling his feet, waiting to be called inside, not hearing Essie's prophetic words.

"The last," Essie uttered, as a fully formed Reave slid into the midwife's huge hands. "Hosea. It means salvation. It means I can stop."

Sepsis stopped Essie a week later, and she settled down next to Gideon for eternity, with only a nameless stone to mark her passing. Admah had good intentions, but sentiment had little leeway with the clan after the last threat of frost, when the furrows waited for peanuts.

Admah handed Hosea over to a new mother in the clan to wet-nurse, went back to the fields, and brooded over the loss of Essie, a woman who never talked back.

CHAPTER FOURTEEN

SECOND BRIDE

G rief was never a fixation for a Reave. Forty acres of prime bottomland was. Abner Reave had no reservations about bursting unannounced into his son's lean-to on a Friday night, five years after Essie's death.

With his shock of white hair standing on end above wild eyes, Abner increasingly resembled the deranged John Brown—though his message was personal, not political. Five years as a widower was unfathomable in the Reave clan, where procreation was an edict from God.

"Opportunity of a lifetime, Admah! My second cousin Saul, the one who lives so high and mighty up by Hickory Creek—married a town gal like you did—talked to me today when I took the eggs into town. He's got a gal just turned fifteen. He says some no-account boys keep hangin' around like ruttin' dogs. He wants her settled. He's got forty acres that runs along the end of our property, just t'other side of the creek. He said a good husband for Wilmy could earn it."

Hosea Reave sat squat, myopic, and sullen, watching his grandfather. Abner glanced over at him. Everyone called the boy "Hoser." It seemed to fit. All traces of Essie Holt had vanished in this ill-kept hut. Filthy bedding, pots with congealed grease, and two unwashed Reaves offended and inspired Abner.

"You got to snap out of it, Admah. This place is a pigsty. Two things matter to a Reave: family and land. You do a disservice to Essie's memory when you don't plan for Hoser's future," Abner flinched with the lie. Thoughts of Essie had retreated into a past of miscellany, none of it very memorable.

"Hoser needs a woman to look after him. Forty acres next to the creek could be a godsend in this kind of drought. Essie would want that for Hoser. She was a practical woman. She gave her life for this boy." He patted Hoser's head quickly, thinking that his pit-bull jaw looked just this side of a snap.

Admah's blank face looked up at his father, as though the threat of drought hadn't registered. The mention of Essie had. With his heavy brow, ditch-colored eyes, and bandy legs, Hoser was a complete throwback to the Reaves. Nothing of Essie resided there, except a kind of sharp expression in his eyes when he was crossed.

Abner had longed for a golden grandchild. Admah missed the blue of Essie's eyes. He stared at his grandson's sulky face bent over a Big Chief lined tablet.

His grandfather asked, "What are you drawing, Hoser? Animals?" Hoser beamed and held up the page for his father and grandfather to admire. Crude as the drawings were, they were inventive. Dogs fornicated with large women. Horses plunged into the back end of small sheep. Women's breasts of all shapes and sizes strung along the top of the page like paper lanterns.

Admah's voice sounded like a thunderclap after a long, dry spell. "I'll do it, Pa. I'll meet Saul's girl. I'll do it for Hoser. He needs a woman's touch."

He needs a belting, thought Abner. "I don't think I'd give him any more drawing materials," Abner tossed over his shoulder, as he headed out the door with an uneasy sense that Hoser knew the drawings were peculiarly interesting to him. He'd stop by the church and pray. Best to pray about Hoser's future. A parcel of land might not satisfy his bestial tendencies.

Hoser first caught sight of his new stepmother, Wilmy, when she swung out of her father's 1959 Ford Ranchero, stretching a plump, chalky leg down further and further, as her knee-length white crepe wedding dress slid up past all imagining.

Wilmy felt the back seam of her too-tight dress giving way, as she angled her body backwards, hung onto the Ford's window post, and fought for purchase on the sandy soil where the Ford's oversized tires rested.

She found purchase on a living, breathing animal and shrieked at the top of her lungs.

"Get up from there, Hoser! You makin' a spectacle." Abner Reave, wearing a curled-brim homburg that had not seen the light of day since he married Admah's mother, yanked his grandson up by one arm and shoved him toward Wilmy. "Meet yore new mama-to-be."

Wilmy winced as she stared at the boy in Abner's grip. His thick lips lapping over skewed teeth gave him the look of a crafty peasant—older than his five years—like one of those Bruegel figures dancing at a country wedding. Or, he might have been a troll from one of those old-fashioned fairy tale books designed to frighten children into good behavior.

Someone had scrubbed his face to a high, reddish sheen. He wore a stiff, new shirt with the store creases still in it. The front of his shirt and knees of his pants were covered with dirt.

In this alien community where a passel of Reaves stood like a line of zombies staring mutely at her in her new wedding finery, this young boy had the kindest eyes she had seen since her daddy locked her in her room until she agreed to marry Admah Reave. With a red hat, this boy would look just like the plaster gnome her mama put out next to the plastic flamingos.

"He was making a stoop for me. I was having trouble getting down from the truck with this dress 'n everythin'. He put hisself right down where I needed to step. I never seen a more hepful boy."

Wilmy grabbed Hoser's grubby hand, lifted her chin and marched toward the line of new relations, their unsmiling faces lining the portico of an otherwise plain, boxy church.

CHAPTER FIFTEEN

THE HELP

Hephzibah Kiel's ancestors came as slaves to Wolfe County with the Chickasaws—before the Civil War. When Edward Posey bought prime bottomland, an assortment of shacks peppered his lands. Generations of the children of slaves stayed on land that had passed from Chickasaw owner-ship to new owners, with no one questioning tenant rights to cabins, sheds, and a few acres for chickens, a cow, and a garden.

The tenants dared not stretch the questionable ownership of their land beyond squatter's rights; they kept their hogs pinned in the willow breaks. They worked as field hands for cash money when the crops were good. Even in lean times, there was corn for the animals and for grinding into cornmeal.

If personal bearing suggested a privileged class, Hephzibah should have been "born to the Purple." Her 220 pounds attached themselves gracefully to her stiff-as-a-rod spinal column; they knelt at her command to scrub floors in endlessly circular patterns; they bolted upright before Miz Lilymae could parcel out menial tasks.

Although she had been the only servant and cook in her father's house—having never given an order to another human—Lilymae Posey was riled to discover a servant in her new Queen Anne house, who managed to stay a task ahead of anything that needed doing.

Long after Hephzibah had become such a household fixture that Lilymae often forgot she was in the room, Lilymae would remember to resent her. She was fond of saying: "Edward proposed to me, but he *chose* Hephzibah."

Annabel remembered that she and her brother Eliot would sit with zippered lips, grateful down to the last quivering atoms in their bodies that their petulant mother had been supplanted by a woman who could smack down a coiled rattlesnake or whip up a lemon meringue pie with the same insouciance.

If not born *to the purple*, Hephzibah was born purple, blue-black as an eggplant, her skin gleaming with the iridescence of a dragonfly's wings. From Annabel's first waking moment, it was Hephzibah bending over her that she would always remember.

Edward Posey had found her in a watermelon patch. At least that's what Hephzibah told Annabel and Eliot. "I warnt no field hand. I been schooled in cooking by Bessie Martingale since I wuz thirteen years. Old Mr. Justinian Wolfe's cook." She would wave distractedly in the direction of Wolfe's Valley where the Wolfes still held court in their Victorian mansion.

"When Mr. Justinian passed, his chile Miss Venetia say she cain't take my sass. More'n ten years in that kitchen, in what do I get for my trouble. Miss Venetia herding me out the do like sum dumb animal."

Hephzibah looked resignedly at her pale tan palms. "I growed callouses big as taters on my hands in them fields afore your pa come to fetch me. Miss Pauline, the good twin, tole him I wuz the best cook in Wolfe County." She'd smile down at Annabel and Eliot with big, white teeth, and remind them of her value. "Yore pa grew up with kitchen hep who know grits gotta cook all day. He particular about such things."

Annabel recalled how carefully Hephzibah avoided any comments about their mother, as she segmented the ways of the world for them—the good from the bad. Her list was legion, a vast compilation that was part Biblical, part Amos 'n' Andy, and the advice of her grandmother, whose mother had been a slave of a well-fixed Chickasaw family in the county.

When they were older, Eliot and Annabel tried to sort out her list. They could identify the Beatitudes and knew that the Kingfish's get-rich-quick schemes didn't come from the mouth of Paul. A few odd things popped up on the list from time to time, something about how they should not make poison from buck-eyes or use green walnut hulls to drug fish when they weren't biting.

They should remember to always bury their dead to face east so they would meet Jesus face to face. The old Chickasaw ritual of putting red stain on a dead person's face might be considered a heathenish prac-tice. But, Hephzibah said it would ensure that the dead person went to the "highest sky."

Annabel warmed with remembrances of her old friend. Hephzibah's list had assured her and Eliot that their world was well ordered—and their moth-er's constant carping had nothing to do with them or their father.

"Miz Lilymae got one of her bad eyeball aches. I taken her a crushed mint poultice. She be better by supper."

She always was, up and about by the time their father finished his rounds of the fields and his busi-ness dealings in Wolfe Flats.

Annabel could recall her mother sitting on the edge of a straight-backed Queen Anne chair, posed like a resurrected Bourbon queen, her skin pale as a marble effigy.

Eyeball headaches be dammed. It was her mother's watchword to greet her husband at the end of the day, even if she didn't seem particularly happy to see him.

With her hair marcelled into tight little waves that accented her high forehead, and a crepe de Chine blouse caressing her swan-like throat, Lilymae played the lady of the manor to the hilt.

After half an hour for cocktails—their father's three fingers of straight bourbon and their mother's lemon water (she had taken the vow of temperance in her father's church), Eliot and Annabel were paraded before their father for the report of their day.

Lilymae had adopted the pattern of formally trotting out their children when she saw photos of a doting King George and his wife fawning over Elizabeth and Margaret at the end of each day, as part of the royal ritual.

Annabel would watch her mother beaming at Eliot, as though he were a prince of the realm, while she listed his good deeds. She would raise her brows condescendingly, as their father asked questions: "Who left the door to the grain shed open so my best saddle horse foundered?"

Eliot just shuffled his feet and looked longingly at their father's bourbon. Annabel should have known that was a sign of things to come. She would simply plop down in front of her father's chair, so he could rake his fingers through her hair. He never seemed to mind that it was stringy and the color of a mouse.

"What did my girl do today?" Annabel knew that her mother would be twitching to tell him about lost opportunities and minor indiscretions, as her slipper convulsed against the pouty foot of the Queen Anne chair.

"Ripped the side out of her new dress before Rhoda finished hemming it. It's the only decent thing she has to wear when we go to Joe Bob's christening. Annabel has outgrown *everything* this summer." The angst in her mother's voice, with the thought of her daughter's leg length or girth, was palpable.

"Surely Rhoda can sew up the side of a dress before Sunday. Who is Joe Bob? And why are we going to his christening?"

That would divert her mother and put her on defense at the same time. In restrospect, Annabel realized that her father was a master of digressions. Joe Bob Cantrell was the infant son of Lilymae's new best friend in the Methodist Church Missionary Society.

Edward Posey never set foot in the Methodist Church. He took his children to the nearest Episcopal church, twenty miles south in Gainesville, for the Eucharist once a month. Lilymae had been married by an Episcopal priest and had studied the required doctrine—a prerequisite for marrying into the Posey family.

In Wolfe Flats, Methodism ruled. Lilymae returned to the fold, hoping for a heady confrontation with Edward over her reclaimed religious heritage. Years into their marriage, she had grown to loathe Edward's tolerance of her—something in his self-assured face, the way he turned it politely toward her when she spoke, as though he knew nothing she had to say would alter the blankness there.

With the persistence of an invisible itch mite burrowing under the skin, Lilymae managed to get a rise out of her husband in two ways: rudeness to his tenants or disrespect to his blood kin. Since her husband's family lived three states away, Lilymae was forced to send her barbed comments toward his tenants until a wrinkled letter from her husband's brother arrived on the June 23, 1940—the same day that Hitler postured in front of the Eiffel Tower.

CHAPTER SIXTEEN

FLESH AND BLOOD

The letter from Edward's older brother said that their cousin Hiram had been confined to the TB sanitarium in Alto, Georgia, and was not improving as hoped. Annabel watched her father's eyes become feverishly bright reading the letter, as though the mycobacteria might have traveled through the postal service.

Her mother affirmed her anxiety: "He's infectious!" she snorted.

"He's kin," her father snarled back, in one of his rare outbursts.

"Distant kin!" she had screeched as Annabel's father headed toward the phone in the hall to make arrangements for his cousin and wife to travel by train to Wolfe Flats.

"Do you remember that tacky Georgette crepe thing Maudie wore to our wedding? Her panels flapping all about after she drank too much punch. No one in *my* family behaved like that!"

Annabel intercepted an almost sinister look that her father sent in her mother's direction, but his voice was controlled. "Your Methodist guests avoided the punch while your father lectured our priest on the sin of popery."

As he picked up the sturdy black handset and dialed the operator, his voice rang out as though he were shouting all the way to Georgia or to no one in particular: "I believe that Mr. Dickens nailed the issue when he said: 'Accidents will occur in the best-regulated families.'"

The debate had concluded; the carping had just begun. The threat of a deadly bacillus just waiting to invade their children's lungs suggested that their mother had won round one; in fact, Edward Posey had immediately begun refurbishing the overseer's house and deeded one hundred acres of good bottomland to his cousin.

The Oklahoma Poseys were short on relatives— no Poseys ventured far from Georgia during those years when the boll weevil and the Great Depression decimated the land. Wolfe County suffered the same drought and falling agricultural prices as the rest of the Midwest and Southern states—painful years, as neighbors watched other neighbors piling into old pickups and heading west toward hope.

Annabel's father owned gins and seed houses; his cotton broker skills served him and his tenants well. Although the economy was rebounding, Lilymae had the heart of a hoarder, always braced for hard times.

She dangled the letter between her thumb and forefinger. "Hitler is in Paris. It was on the morning news. We'll all be darning our socks and turning our collars before this is over. You cannot be *magnanimous* at a time like this, Edward." Her mouth darkened and puckered into a raisin.

Annabel remembered how her father's face radiated the moment her mother drawled out "*magnanimous.*" Dropping the black receiver back into position, he beamed down at his children. "Our family has been too small—just us and Hephzibah. Now we'll have Hiram and Maudie watching out for us. That's what families do. Watch out for each other." The glance he shot his wife suggested that he might be offering her a definition of family that was entirely foreign to her.

Two weeks later, the day that Hiram and Maudie Posey were to arrive at the Wolfe Flats Depot sometime around mid-afternoon, Lilymae archly announced across the breakfast table: "Mrs. Simpson hosts bridge club today. I'll need the Chevrolet. I let one of your tenants borrow the pickup yesterday. I forgot to tell you. Give my regards to your cousin."

In 1940, two-car families in Wolfe Flats were nonexistent. Annabel recalled her flush of embarrassment as her father harnessed two mules to the old Linsgtroth wagon. She and Eliot followed him into town on their ponies with an unspoken sense of shame for their mother's rudeness.

Only families from the West End rode into town in wagons. Poseys did not meet relatives at the depot behind a team of mules. Years later, remembering the wagon lurching along the road, Annabel would recall her mother's wry summary of her marriage: "Your father and I were out of sync, like unbalanced wheels on a wagon. It goes. It does the job. It's just not a pretty thing to watch."

Their nonplussed father had spotted the train slowing and slapped the reins to speed up the mules. Pulling up the wagon in front of the blacksmith shop next to the depot, he flung himself down, whipped the reins over one of the few hitching posts left in town, and charged into a small group of passengers who had just descended.

Annabel stared at a very tall man with cavernous eyes who clutched her father's thin body, as though it had become a lifeline. When they moved apart, the man seemed to shrink into himself, as though conscious that he might be taking up too much space. The arc of his back formed such a gentle curve that his head jutted forward like a turtle, with the same wise and searching eyes.

"Eliot. Annabel. Meet your cousins, Hiram and Maudie." A pale, sausage-shaped arm peeled out of a skin-tight sleeve and wrapped itself snugly about Annabel's shoulders. The affection startled her.

She pulled away quickly and peered into the doughy face of Cousin Maudie. As a six-year-old literalist, Annabel sometimes repeated exactly what she heard. "Mother says you're a double first cousin of Cousin Hiram." Just as she added, "Mother says double first cousins shouldn't marry," she felt her father's pinch.

His eyes hooded dangerously without releasing his grip on her arm, so she announced to no one in particular, "Edgar Poe married his cousin, and Father named me for the girl in his poem." Her father's grip was as effective as a twitch on a horse's mouth. She stared at her feet, not sure why her information was met with this uncomfortable silence.

She could see Eliot glowering at her, as he made a fuss about sorting out bags and carrying them to the wagon. Her father ignored her and made a production of hoisting Maudie up to a springy wagon seat that just might collapse under her hips.

Annabel remembered the hot tears that sprang to her eyes. She had been trying to make up for the fact that her mother had chosen her bridge club over greeting her relatives by saying exactly what her mother had said, filling in for her, so to speak.

At that moment, she felt herself being swung out, as though she weighed no more than a feather, and then back before being settled gently onto her saddle. The voice that whispered above her came from very far up: "It was many and many a year ago in a kingdom by the sea that a maiden there lived that you may know by the name of Annabel Lee."

Hiram Posey watched the tearful eyes of the sturdy little girl brighten in relief. She kneed her horse forward until it bumped her brother. Eliot shot her a carefully tempered grin.

That grin triggered a dozen memories of his cousin Edward as a boy. As favorite cousins, they did everything together. Then Edward went away to college, and Hiram tried to salvage his father's unprofitable real estate along the railroad corridors in Atlanta.

He ended up salvaging Maudie, the daughter of an uncle that his father had sweet-talked into investing in his failing business. In her youth, Maudie gave a new meaning to the term "Georgia peach"—a fleshy girl radiating good health and good will in spite of her family's misfortunes. The war had claimed her family's two plantations, a general store, half a dozen cotton gins, and the left leg of her grandfather.

Hiram peered up at the sorely tested wagon seat holding his wife. Maudie beamed down at him and flashed another smile at his cousin. Gratitude tempered the space around Maudie. She couldn't imagine pretending to be anything but exactly what she was. She was nothing like Lilymae Macabee.

The Poseys gossiped about this daughter of a Methodist preacher who had enthralled Edward. His resettlement to Oklahoma wasn't surprising, but his choice of a bride was.

Hiram and Edward had talked at length about the "miasma" of the South. Edward had the means to leave; Hiram had only foreclosures and a troop of Maudie's poor relations.

From his view, as best man, by Edward's side near the altar at St. Luke's, the bride coming up the aisle had dazzled Hiram—her russet hair the only splash of color against skin as pale as the silk she wore. In the reception line, he noted her sharp eyes sizing up Maudie's new dress and her lids blinking like numbers on an old crank-operated cash register, as she gauged the social standing of the wedding guests.

No sale. *Mene, mene, tekel upharsin.* Weighed in thy balances and found wanting. Lilymae had swished her bridal train that was the length of the West Point Route behind her, sometimes causing her husband to stumble, as she clung like a vine to Edward, making his way around the room to greet his friends and relatives.

Hiram thought about the noxious Kudzu that had invaded Georgia, the way it takes over and smothers everything that comes within its tendrils. It is an *intentional* plant that thrives like gorse out of its native territory. The expression in the new Mrs. Posey's eyes was full of intent.

Now, outside this depot in Wolfe Flats, his cousin Edward hung fire before his eyes, a stalled, thin-as-a-snake man who had aged too quickly around the eyes. No. In the eyes.

The cut of his jacket and the ease with which he accommodated a cousin-by-marriage that he had briefly met, years before, marked Edward Posey as the same self-assured, the-world-is-my-apple person he had always been. The eyes were different—eminently sad, as though he had Billie Holiday's "Gloomy Sunday" playing over and over in his head.

When Edward had called him at the sanitorium, he asked Hiram to come live in Wolfe County, almost begged him, as though their fortunes had been reversed. His single, plaintive request had sealed the deal: "I need *avuncular* protection for my children. I need you."

Hiram glanced over at Edward's children—an uncertain little girl with kindness in her eyes that didn't come from her mother and that Byronic boy without a single, obvious, physical flaw.

Both of the children seemed to have a need to be in control—Eliot single-handedly hoisting baggage into the wagon and Annabel with her odd pronouncements. Yet, there was an air of edginess about them; the way that Annabel pulled away when Maudie had hugged her startled him. The children moved in unison like identical twins do when they think no one is looking, as though a singular act might diminish them.

CHAPTER SEVENTEEN

BAD NEWS

I n mid-May, the fields of wild clover shoving heedlessly against Wolfe Flats Elementary School sent waves of the scent of summer into the industrial-sized windows of Annabel's fourth-grade classroom where twenty-five restless children quivered in anticipation of freedom.

When Principal Edwards tiptoed into the room that afternoon and whispered to the teacher, Annabel stood without being beckoned. She could see her pale-faced brother standing in the hall. They followed the principal outside to his pudgy, gray Plymouth, whose waterfall grille seemed to be leering at them, aware of a misfortune that had not been named.

"Your mother asked me to bring you home," he blurted out, swinging the heavy door wide.

"Why?" Eliot's whisper was hardly audible.

"Not for me to say. She'll tell you. You tell her how sorry I am."

The conundrum solved itself when their mother met them on the front porch wearing a black satin dress that suggested a cocktail party was in the offing.

"He's in the parlor. Passed on just after you got on the school bus. Went like that." She snapped her fingers for emphasis and moved regally ahead of her children, with a bowed head, like Victoria mourning her beloved Albert.

Their mother didn't fool them. The games had begun. Annabel could see the ugly shape of the box with its ornate and useless brass handles. Billows of white satin hid the hinges of a lid that would close on her father forever; his expression was grim, as though he had met his maker and wasn't pleased with the acquaintance.

Eliot refused to come near the casket. Within the hour, he had dragged a large pile of logs and sticks into the rose garden and positioned a redwood chaise lounge atop it.

Watching Hiram carrying her brother, his legs dangling like an unstrung puppet, through thick prairie grasses to his home in the overseer's old house, Annabel knew exactly why Eliot had built the pyre. Their father should go out of this world in a blaze, like a Viking warrior—not encased in a satin-lined box inside a borrowed church.

If anyone could mediate her brother's grief, it would be Cousin Hiram. Her mother's fury over the smashed roses would be redirected to Annabel, who crept into Hephzibah's bed and wept until the cock crowed.

Edward's funeral rekindled feelings for him that Lilymae had not experienced since sasheying around their wedding tent in Atlanta, knowing that all eyes were on her. That day, she had experienced optimism for the first time that she could remember.

During the funeral, a faint whiff of hopefulness had returned. The eulogies by Edward's friends celebrated someone she faintly remembered, like a hastily invited dinner guest whose name one can't recall. The Anglican priest from Gainesville, trailing his skirts down the aisle of a borrowed Methodist church, and those discordant, unfamiliar hymns formed a backdrop to her elegant, feigned misery.

Edward made a fine show for a dead man. Mouth sealed. Collar starched nicely. Tie a perfect choice for the gray suit. For once, her children were solemn. Her son's remarkably handsome profile did her credit. Annabel's puffy eyes were only marginally less attractive than her sallow skin. The color of mourning did nothing for her complexion. On the bright side, thought Lilymae, Annabel was not a distraction to her mother's new state of suffering.

The black of widowhood suited Lilymae. To keep up appearances, she ordered new mourning outfits from Neiman-Marcus. She erected a black granite edifice that it could be seen half a mile from Lakeview Cemetery—marginally shorter than the Royal Arch Mason structure over Vernica Robert's father.

The house reeked with the stench of decaying lilies so that callers would be impressed by the "tributes." Until her husband's will was read, a week after his funeral, Lilymae postured for the community while she plotted against everyone who had failed to respect her—the soon-to-be landless tenants, those hanger-ons, Hiram and Maudie, and her children's devoted Hephzibah, who would be sent packing back to her tepee.

CHAPTER EIGHTEEN

ISOSCELES TRIANGLES

If Lilymae Posey could have chosen a family motto, it would have come from Auden's comment about the "fascinating class of which I am the only member."

Convinced that her early widowhood marked her as both tragic and noble, Lilymae went about Wolfe Flats with her left hand hovering just above her heart, a stricken Victoria. Her grief—when it materialized—couched itself in rancorous attacks on her husband's tenants.

Before the reading of the will, Lilymae swept into the front parlor amidst waves of black silk that did nothing to mediate the rapacious expression on her face. The grieving widow propped a child on each side of her, sent disdainful looks toward Hiram and Hephzibah, and practiced little speeches in her mind about how quickly Edward's cousin and tacky wife would be dispatched—and how the disrespectful Hephzibah would pack her bag by evening.

Edward Posey had foreseen the havoc his unbridled wife might wreck on a community he had so carefully cultivated. His will sorted out everything. His cousin Hiram would manage the farms. Lawyers and CPAs would manage everything else, until Eliot and Annabel came of age.

The stinger in the will that enraged Lilymae insured that Eliot and Annabel would come of age with a safety net. For continuing to assist with the "tending and care" of his beloved children "as previously discussed," both Hiram and Hephzibah received sizeable bequests.

In accordance with his client's wishes, Edward Posey's lawyer made sure that his children stayed in the room with the other beneficiaries as the will was read.

Earlier that morning, Annabel remembered that her mother had almost gleefully made comments about "shirt-tailed relatives" and "hired help getting above themselves."

"She delights in schadenfreude, Annabel. The misfortunes of others send Mother into a state of bliss," Eliot had blurted out as their mother headed up to the attic that morning to look for an old suitcase "in case Hephzibah needed one." On the day after his funeral, Eliot had moved their father's twelve-volume set of the OED into his room and tried out a new word on Annabel every day.

"She's out to get Cousin Hiram and Maudie. Probably won't keep Hephzibah around either." Twelve-year-old boys weren't supposed to cry, but Annabel could see the red rims around Eliot's eyes— as though he had been secretly crying for days.

Although their father named his cousin Hiram to act as a guardian for his children, their mother would determine how things would be for *her* children. Within a year, their beloved Hephzibah would crawl outside to die under a tree, leaving only Hiram to mediate in their behalf.

The year of her father's death, the radio blasted the news of Japanese trapping Americans in the Bataan Peninsula, the Red Army in retreat, and bombs flashing like Roman candles, as though the entire world were unraveling, not just Annabel's cosmos.

Years later, Annabel remembered herself as a ten-year-old whose father had died too soon and travelled too fast into his grave, ending forever what had been her safe world, as the spooks installed themselves with her mother.

Edward had been settled into his grave for only two weeks when one of the women in Lilymae's bridge group brought her a battered Ouija board so she could commune with the spirit of her dead husband.

Like the persistent clicking of knitting needles, the pointer on her mother's Ouija board tapped into the paranormal at night. "Are you there, Edward? Are you on the other side? Do you have your human shape? How will I know you?"

Annabel longed to shout through the bedroom wall: "You didn't know him in this life, Mother. How could you expect to recognize him in another?"

Instead, she pulled the blanket over her head, her silence indefatigable. It's what she learned to practice after her father died; she could show everyone that her dull ache had disappeared, because she and Eliot no longer mattered to anyone.

Except Hephzibah and Cousin Hiram. On the day that the Allies bombed the sacred city of Rome, Hephzibah failed to put the coffee on to boil. No biscuits bloomed in the oven. No sound came from her sleeping porch off the kitchen.

Eliot found her propped up under the Hackberry tree on the north side of the house and ran to get Annabel. "Her breathing is ragged. She looks sick. I wanted to get Mother, but Hephzibah told me to bring only you. She said it was time for us to remember what we promised."

They remembered. The viewing was set in Goodin's Funeral Parlor the day before the Methodist church service. In attendance were a grandson from Ardmore, fifteen Methodists, Hiram and Maudie, and Lilymae and her children. Hephzibah's broad, kind, coffee-colored face would be seen no more—as she had insisted. Her traditional funeral at the Methodist church would have a non-traditional, closed casket.

After the all-day viewing in Goodin's before the funeral, that night Annabel and Eliot had ridden their ponies into Wolfe Flats and hitched them behind the funeral parlor. It was a sullen July night with the kind of darkness that encouraged nightjars to crouch defiantly in the center of the road to spook horses and jittery children.

Clutching a glass jar of canned beets, Eliot eased open the back door and pulled Annabel behind him down a spooky hallway into a room that smelled of talcum and death. The moon flashed a thin beam of light through an upper window onto a gleaming wooden box that their mother had called a "sarcophagus—and too fancy by far for hired help."

"Jes dump it on me," Hephzibah had whispered hoarsely from her propped position under the Hackberry when she saw Lilymae rounding the house. "Don't have to touch no dead person. Dump 'n run. Jes like we talked."

Like two small acolytes preparing for the celebrant, they dipped their fingers in beet juice and smoothed the color all about the face of the woman they had loved more than they could ever love their mother. Her face was cool to the touch, strangely still, transmitting calmness as it always had.

"If we were doing it right, we'd bury her sitting up under the house, under her sleeping porch. That's the old Chickasaw way. That's what she said," Eliot whispered.

"She took the Jesus road, Eliot. Father bought her a place in the cemetery just to the right of his grave."

"That will piss off Mother," Eliot's voice was too loud; he folded over the casket lid and clicked the latches in place.

Those were the last words of the evening. Eliot thumped his pony into a gentle lope ahead of Annabel. Under a pale sliver of the moon, she could see his shoulders heaving. Whether in grief for their beloved Hephzibah or pleasure in anticipating Lilymae's frozen face at the gravesite she would never know.

CHAPTER NINETEEN

COPING

L ilymae bloomed in the atmosphere of mourning; black garments set her pale skin and russet
hair in sharp relief, like the image on an old tintype.
Having forgotten to clip a lock of her husband's hair
for a Victorian-style mourning brooch, Lilymae
was reduced to pulling strands of hair from his cel-
luloid hairbrush and substituting a fuzzy clump in
an antique gold and black enameled ornament that
once housed a stranger's silvery strands.

Unlike the widowed queen she so admired, Lilymae Posey could not bring herself to retreat into grief.
Restricted from meddling in the business of her husband's estate, she muscled in on her children's lives
like a sumo wrestler clearing the ring of all opponents.

Opposition festered like an abcess when Eliot
refused to kiss the clammy face of his father. Acceding

to her mother's pleading for "how it must look" left Annabel with the imprint of her father's dead flesh on her lips and in her dreams.

Watching the tremor pass through his sister like a tectonic plate as she bent over their father's unnaturally pink face left Eliot with the nagging certainty that he was born to break rules—not the big ones on Moses' tablet, but little ones, the kind that would annoy his mother worse than coveting his neighbor's maidservant or ass.

These would be the questionable rules, such as coming in second just before the finish line, opting for salutatorian when he could be valedictorian, skipping classes so that a four-year baccalaureate would take six—annoying his mother like a persistent, untreatable case of scabies.

Annabel watched Eliot maneuvering like a slippery Houdini in opposing his mother's influence. He sailed through high school effortlessly, like one of those engaging clipper ships, facile and lazy, but over-canvassed for high winds. His mother claimed that Eliot was destined for an exceptional life. She didn't have to remind Annabel that she was destined for no life at all.

For all his nonchalant airs, Annabel knew that Eliot was growing up under a veil of absolutism. Like a young dauphin, Eliot carried the weight of an only son and the Posey heir.

It was his mother's fantasy that their Wolfe County property had transmogrified into a plantation from *Gone with the Wind*. She imagined Eliot as a young Ashley Wilkes being worshiped by his tenants, watching their work from afar, princely and aloof.

Eliot saw himself only as a co-worker, driving his father's old pickup to the fields, and working cattle with anyone who needed an extra hand. He went to school with the sons of their tenants and leapt bare-assed with them into Red River. He ate with their families. Too often, according to his mother.

A year after her husband's death, Lilymae determined that Eliot needed "more refined companions," as she plopped brochures of private schools beside his breakfast plate.

"Not going, Mother. Not. I'll go away to college, but I'm staying in high school with my friends. Cousin Hiram agrees. End of discussion." His face took on a murderous tint as he planted yet another four-color brochure in his scrambled eggs. Annabel took secret pleasure in watching her brother divert their mother from her beaten path.

Not for long. Their mother had a message to deliver to the world about her gifted son. Doing the work of the three fates, she spun Eliot's past, present, and future into a tapestry of her own making, putting row upon row of photographs of Eliot's journey along the entry hall wall. Instead of a tapestry embroidered with multiple kings, battles, and corpses, Lilymae's tapestry was designed to keep Eliot on the throne.

Nevertheless, he fell off frequently. Annabel remembered the night during his senior year when

Eliot plowed his car through their mother's rose bed. Oklahoma was a dry state, but her brother could always find hooch. Around midnight, she heard him struggling with the front door and hurried downstairs before he woke their mother.

Sprawled on the porch with a mess of yellowish, clotted gunk on his shirt, Eliot smiled crookedly and pointed up at the canopy of bright stars. "'Lo, Annabel. And the stars never rise but I feel the bright eyes of the beautiful Annabel Lee."

"Why do you do this, Eliot?" His sister looked at his car mired in the roses. "She'll be furious."

"Not with her golden boy, not our sainted mother. She'll find a way to make someone else pay." He hiccupped loudly and pulled himself up to squat on the plinth. "Probably Cousin Hiram for not putting a wall around her roses."

He pushed himself into an upright position and grimaced at the mess on his shirt. "Choc beer. Have to strain the chicken feed out with your teeth. A civilized state wouldn't be dry. We should have gone across the river to one of the joints, but Jewel Fay swiped a gallon of her daddy's choc."

"You weren't with Jewel Fay! She's a . . . a . . ." Annabel paused, considering the lesser evil in Jewel Fay's minor order of sins: Lana Turner breasts under a tight red sweater or—as her mother would declare—white trash.

"She's a girl who knows how to have fun and can drink me under the table any day of the week. She has very low expectations and a fine sense of balance. *She didn't fall off the water tower tonight.*"

He held up a wrist that angled oddly to one side and muttered, "Better go get Maudie to splint this. I'm about to . . ." He passed out effortlessly, stretching his body into one of those stiff poses, like an effigy on a tomb, her handsome, charming, doomed brother.

The Gods had blessed Eliot with beauty and brains. The surfeit had sickened him. Annabel remembered running across the field that night to bang on Cousin Hiram's door. As she ran, she prayed to her father's Anglican god, who tolerated liquor, that her brother would survive the summer and come to his senses at Harvard.

He became more like himself at Harvard. That first Christmas at home, Eliot hopped off the train with his hair brushed back from his forehead in an Alexander's "quiff," or *anastole*, as the Greeks called it, and the strong scent of whiskey on his breath. He regaled Annabel and his mother with stories of varsity rowing on the Charles River. He had taken up mountain climbing and peppered his speech with terms like "carabiners" and "roping down."

Annabel remembered flipping through the photo album that he gave her for Christmas and thinking that Eliot had adopted other Alexandrian habits, like keeping "women and eunuchs in tow." Faces clustered like daisy petals around a golden center that was

Eliot. Young women smiled with dark lips, a sure sign of bright red lipstick in those black and white photos. Annabel noted, curiously, that some of the men in his theater group grinned with similar dark lips.

Before his tricky aorta sprung a leak, their father had talked to Eliot and Annabel about their "formative years," about reading good books and learning from the past. She wondered how their father would view Eliot's role model. Alexander's daring was admirable, his deeds often catastrophic.

With Eliot safely tucked into the end of a sophomore year at Harvard that might stretch out into infinity as he skirted the minimum four courses per term, Lilymae determined to take a firmer hand with her daughter.

Either Wellesley or Smith would do, so that Eliot could look in on his sister. In defiance of her mother, Annabel had sent only one application to Southeastern State College, less than an hour's drive from Wolfe Flats.

Lilymae would have the summer to work on her daughter, a child so compliant that she had been easy to neglect. An elaborate graduation party would compensate for all those birthdays remembered only when Hiram showed up with a gift and one of Maudie's cakes, oozing with calories forbidden to Annabel.

CHAPTER TWENTY

COMMENCEMENT

Annabel's entire graduating class and all of her teachers gathered under a tent on the Posey lawn to shuffle on a prefab dance floor, as a mediocre band from Ardmore imported "The Tennessee Waltz" to Wolfe Flats.

Lilymae adopted a military posture by the punch bowl to prevent foreign products from being added to the mixture; she smiled and waved to guests with what she considered to be queenly elegance in a Don Loper cocktail dress, red—not black—for her daughter's special night.

The billows of net skirting—costing a fraction of Lilymae's Loper fashion statement—did nothing for her sturdily built daughter's figure, but the Helms boy didn't appear to notice, as he hobbled from a waltz to a two-step without marking the difference in the beat.

After a brief fracus on the floor with that boorish classmate of theirs, Orville Bemis, both Annabel and Willie Helms had disappeared—for too long. Lilymae finally sent him packing after all the other guests had gone.

The next morning over breakfast, Lilymae cast a gimlet eye at her daughter. "I hope you have better judgment than to waste your time on local boys. I had assumed that they wouldn't be attracted to a plain girl. Older men or fortune hunters may be another matter. A clever girl like you *might* find someone worthy. Later. After you've done college—back East."

Her pronouncement sounded like a benediction to Annabel. Willie wasn't a fortune hunter. Willie was worthy.

Worthy as he might have been, Annabel reflected much later, Willie's life had veered off course—as did his parents' pickup on that icy highway. Her own life had stayed the course; she had become an anachronism, a remnant from the late Nineteenth Century, one of those stay-at-home spinsters frittering away her life.

Four years at Southeastern State College prepared her to teach; nothing could prepare her for the machinations of her mother to keep her out of a classroom once Lilymae got wind of the fact that Annabel had switched her major from art to education.

"Poseys do not teach in public schools. You can write something or draw little animals like that Potter woman. You used to sketch. Or, you can grow herbs. You can be on committees, that sort of thing. You get along with people." Lilymae looked askance at her daughter. "That cafeteria at your college must cook with lard. Just look at the way you've filled out, Annabel."

Only her mother's reassurance could top her censure: "You're a plain girl who was born to set a good example. You'll never have to grieve over a man breaking your heart. I warned your father about naming you after that girl in a poem. I was afraid you'd grow up with odd ideas. Edgar Poe was a pedophile. Married his thirteen-year-old cousin. Incest as well," she wrapped her tongue around that spiteful word, enjoying the savor of it.

Years later, Annabel would ponder why she had become exactly what her mother determined she would be—malleable, an almost-but-not top student, always friendly with classmates but not making close friends her own age. She was conciliatory, a girl who smoothed out things.

Annabel saw herself puttering around the edges of her mother's domain like a gardener who plants the same zinnias in the same place year after year. Even during her disobliging years as a teenager, Annabel could never say what she meant. She said what her mother expected her to say or nothing at all. She cured her unhappiness by walking as far as the silo, weeping all the way and dry-eyed on the return trip.

ﻌﻌﻌ

When Annabel prepared to come home to Wolfe Flats after four years in Durant, she possessed a teaching certificate that qualified her to stand in a classroom and talk about the heliocentric universe of Copernicus in front of all the Methodist and Baptist children in Wolfe Flats who knew they hung on the chain of being somewhere between angels and monkeys.

A ninth-grade English teaching position had opened with the forced retirement of Miss Eula Thorndyke who, after fifty-five years of teaching, had begun wearing her corset outside of her dress. Lilymae Posey paid a personal visit to the Superintendent of Wolfe Flats schools to make certain that her daughter would not be a replacement.

For both Eliot and Annabel, being away at college legitimized the desertion of their mother. Eliot's two extra years in Boston doing "theatricals" might have continued had not Cousin Hiram's wife intervened.

"It's the wasting disease!" Maudie shouted on the phone to Annabel, as though the fifty miles to Southeastern State College could be spanned with a raised voice and no telephone line.

When Annabel mustered the will to call Eliot in Boston, he shouted in disbelief: "Wasting disease is what mule deer have. Mother? No way!"

"That's what Maudie told me. Doctor Burney says its *anorexia nervosa*, sort of a mental problem. She won't eat. This is finals week for me, Eliot. I think I may have triggered something a couple of weeks ago by telling Mother that my degree is in education— not art. I didn't want her to be surprised when Hiram drives her over to my graduation. There's an open teaching position in Wolfe Flats. I thought she'd be pleased to have me working close to home. She told me that she'd 'die first'—and she's busy doing it."

Annabel could hear static on the phone, then Eliot's soft drawl: "Mother is back at her games, Annabel. She'll never allow you to teach. She tells people that I'm doing graduate work at Harvard. I'm not. Mother is a master of manipulation. Now she has Maudie stirred up. She's been playing Victoria for so long that she doesn't make a convincing Camille. Stay put. I'm going to."

After her starvation failed to move her children into an obedient mode, a week later, Lilymae Posey rode in a screaming ambulance across the border to Gainesville to have a hot appendix removed. Six days later, both of her children were there for her dismissal, watching their mother as she regally wheeled herself through the hospital lobby, slapping away helpful hands.

The leering grill of Lilymae's azure blue Eldorado self-righteously blocked the emergency entrance, as Eliot bumped his mother's wheelchair down a small ramp.

"Annabel, you get in the back with Hiram. Eliot will chauffeur me home. I'm relieved to be out of that place. Those dreadful white shoes and tacky hats the nurses wear annoyed me more than the odor of carbolic soap. We will all fit nicely if Annabel scrunches up," Lilymae announced autocratically as Hiram swung open the driver's door and folded his tall body awkwardly behind the driver's seat.

"Second law of thermodynamics, Cousin Hiram: the entropy of a closed system can only increase," Eliot grinned slyly at Hiram, as Annabel tried to recall what happens when the vortex is passive but thermodynamics declares it active.

CHAPTER TWENTY-ONE

FINDING HOBBIES

Years after Eliot had given up life in Boston, his pictorial history remained active in the hallway. He beamed through boxy white teeth behind a trophy for the grade-school spelling bee, his top academic achievement. His body arced like a young gladiator's behind a deadly tennis serve.

Smiling young men, arms linked with Eliot always at the center, flanked the photo of him with his Harvard mortarboard atop his head like a crown. The face below appeared a bit hesitant, fearful of what might lie at the end of the tapestry when the threads ran out. It was the last photo that their mother had plastered to the wall.

A baccalaureate from Harvard that took him six years to complete fitted Eliot for a return to "his duties," according to his mother. That meant a portfolio of stocks and bonds that any investment banker could manage better than Eliot—and dealing with the production of tenant farmers who would no longer be his friends.

When she allowed herself to worry about her brother, Annabel reflected ruefully that he did not exactly fulfill the promise that their mother had laid out for him in that parade of old photos.

Annabel's mother had no delusions about her daughter's future. "Now that you've finished with that teacher's college, you'll have plenty to occupy yourself with a few civic duties." Her mother had glanced down the hall at Eliot's tapestry of achievements in black and white. A single photograph of Annabel's graduating class was nailed considerably off-center. Her face, among others, was the size of a pea.

Upon his return from Harvard, Eliot did many things. He wandered about their father's extensive farmlands, glad-handing the tenants, pretending not to notice the sly expressions and locked barns, puzzled by being greeted with a kind of sullen respect—and no invitations to come inside.

By the time he was thirty, Eliot Posey had tested the patience of all the eligible females in Wolfe County, as he darted from woman to woman, like one of those rainbow-colored trout testing lures up and down the stream.

Watching her son fishtail around the crossroads and speed past the regiment of poplar trees lining the long driveway to the house, his mother was still holding out for a "Boston girl from a good family," as she let out a small, audible sigh. "That boy is having trouble settling. It comes of having the kind of arcane beauty that some memorable men, like poets, are blessed with."

Blessed? Annabel glared at her mother, while thinking about disillusioned poets, like Shelley or Byron, who end up in watery graves.

"Watercolors," her mother announced, as if she might be reading Annabel's mind, and added: "For his birthday. Eliot has always been such a talented boy, with strengths yet to be discovered. I just ordered every color of the rainbow in Winsor and Newton paints. Nothing but the best for my son. Also, stacks of paper. You won't believe what that cost. Vernica Roberts will give him lessons. She has nothing better to do after the school board fired her. That nervous breakdown took the wind out of *her* sails."

Annabel refused to respond to her mother's brutal assessment of a long-time family friend—respected by their father and a confidant of his children.

"Don't give me the fish-eye, Annabel. I found your father's affection for that old maid irksome, but to give the devil his due, Vernica's grandmother was a founding member of the DAR. I never fail to offer Vernica the civility of invitations to my social events.

And I offered her a generous payment for Eliot's lessons. Which she refused."

"Lessons? Or money?" Annabel's snarky tone wiped the petulant expression off her mother's face.

"Oh, Vernica said she is more than happy to paint with Eliot," Lilymae's voice became hushed, secretive. "You may not know it, Annabel, but, as a girl, she went to the best art academy in Philadelphia. It cost her grandmother a bundle. One of my bridge ladies let that slip—when we were speculating about what Vernica would do to make herself useful now that she's been ousted from the classroom. That's what got me thinking about a way that she might be useful to Eliot."

Just as the backdoor slammed, Lilymae put a finger to her lips. "Not a word to Eliot. It's a birthday surprise. The art supplies. I've more than repaid Vernica over the years. Heaven only knows how many times she has been a guest at my dinner table."

Annabel was pleased to observe Eliot turning the tables on their mother once again, causing Lilymae considerable regret that she had ever considered painting as a hobby for her son. Vernica Roberts visited twice a week, slapping up her big wooden easel next to Eliot's, talking endlessly to him about Chagall and Matisse—as Lilymae eavesdropped.

Sometimes Annabel eavesdropped as well. Like a nun in a cell, Annabel could imagine only one kind of future for herself—in a classroom. As she watched Vernica brushing swaths of runny colors on thick, absorbant paper, explaining her technique to Eliot, Annabel conjured up a room of inquisitive faces fixated on what she might say as a teacher—if such an opportunity arose.

Whatever she said, Annabel's mythical students probably wouldn't remember it. They might remember her as diligent and respectful—a friend to anyone with an inclination to learn. That's the kind of friend Vernica Roberts had been to her—and to Eliot.

Friendship did not translate into great art. Eliot painted hundreds of watercolors of Oklahoma sunsets, always from the same location on the west-facing porch. "Our own Monet," their mother would exclaim over Eliot's runny pink and orange skies. The Rouen Cathedral was very far away.

While her son dabbled in watercolors and her daughter's maturing face squared itself into a facsimile of her Grandfather Macabee's, Lilymae took on the problem of poltergeists in their house.

She had not dared to mention their presence when her new husband brought her into the magnificently furbelowed Queen Anne, smelling of new lumber and drying varnish.

Spirits preferred old houses, moldy closets, and spider-webbed attics. They must have traveled from Georgia with her. They had been with her since the night that her father yanked up the tiny creature from between her mother's legs, where it lay pulsating in a slimy mess.

He had buried it in the woods with no more ceremony than fear and loathing. Lilymae had seen it in his eyes, heard it in his "spawn of the Devil" words, and watched it as he buried her mother two days later, his face assembled into that of a stricken widower.

In that small wooden church with "Blessed Assurance" ringing to the rafters, the voices of spirits first began whispering in Lilymae's ears: "Mendacity." It was her father's lie, but she had watched it happen. She had remained silent. No spirits would take up with a mettlesome Methodist preacher, but they did move in with his fearful daughter.

Lilymae accepted her connection to the spirit world as a questionable gift, but uniquely hers. As a child, she found it had helped her face the rows of Methodist faces when she passed the offering plate or pounded the piano. Her connection had never brought her a moment of peace or a modicum of truth—just an infernal buzzing in her head.

She had watched her own children for traces of this gift, peered into their eyes when the edge of a rug curled or a candled snuffed itself.

When she heard her husband tumble off the front porch swing that morning in May, she felt the smallest frisson of fear. After the stroke silenced his heart, his face settled into a lopsided rigidity that

Hephzibah, with her compressions to his chest and tears, could not right.

His glassy blue eyes looked straight up into Lilymae's with a single question. The eyes were not unfriendly, just curious, with a question that needed to be answered. For the life of her, Lilymae could not utter a word, as a great silence descended into her head, suddenly bereft of spirits.

CHAPTER TWENTY-TWO

REAVES SPAWN

For the seven years that Wilmy was a virtual prisoner in the Reave compound, her stepson Hoser remained her constant ally. She didn't mind that only a curtain hid the bed where Admah pumped away with the regularity and mindlessness of the generator that Abner hauled next to their lean-to as a wedding present.

The knowing glances that Hoser sent in her direction over the grits and sausage that Admah demanded every morning caused Wilmy no embarrassment. Hoser had become complicit in their small conspiracies to give her life a bit of an edge.

At night, Hoser raided Admah's pockets for small change that he and Wilmy kept in an Acme coffee can, tucked in the lower drawer of the chifferobe.

"If I was a loose woman, one of them that hangs out by Spencer's Hotel in town, I'd be makin' more than a few dimes for my work. You wouldn't understand that Hoser. You're too young."

Hoser understood better than Wilmy could imagine. The next raid on Admah's pocket netted two wrinkled dollar bills.

Siphoning off his Grandfather Abner's hoard of sugar, cup by cup, was a titillating risk. Though rationing was a thing of the past, white sugar was a luxury, meted out from the community storeroom for special occasions and bake sales at the livestock auction barn in Wolfe Flats.

Over the years, the Reave women found bright polyester for their dresses and ways to get their own spending money by selling baked goods to town women.

Except for sausage, grits, and a rabbit stew that could outlast anyone's hunger, Wilmy's one culinary skill was making fudge. Cream and butter and white sugar mixed with cocoa were brought to a boil on a temperamental wood stove that Hoser stoked with corncobs. The secretiveness of the ritual sent both Wilmy and Hoser into fits of stifled giggles.

When bubbles beaded around the top of the heavy cast iron kettle, Hoser would extend half a glass of fresh well water to let Wilmy drip a single thread of syrup into the water. With the tip of one finger, she would prod the lump and whisper: "Ready."

That was Hoser's signal to set to with a large wooden spoon, beating and slapping the molten mass until it was rolled onto a slab, left to harden, and cut into large pieces that they hid from Admah.

As was her habit, Wilmy rolled out of bed into a cool, late fall morning, pulled a roll of sausage from the cooling shelf in the cistern, and patted clumps of raw sausage into patties; she plopped them into a cold, iron skillet, one by one, and immediately vomited.

"What the hell?" Admah shoved aside the drape and scowled at the mess on the floor. Hoser was holding Wilmy's head and sponging off her face, as she continued to gag.

"Wilmy's ailin'n I need to get her to bed. Fix yore own food. I ain't hungry." Hoser's accusatory glare stopped Admah from smacking his cheeky son.

Admah flipped half-burned sausages and watched Wilmy drop onto the rumpled, coarse sheets. Hoser continued to mop her face. She had a greenish cast to her face that was unnaturally white, because she always wore a bonnet in the field.

His first wife, Essie, had that same affectation about the sun on her skin—and the same blanched look when she was going through that alphabet of babies. Seven babies, ill-formed or hardly formed at all, as the contractions came on too soon and too fast.

Then Hoser tore out of her body like an evil imp. Two days later, her heart raced, her fever soared, and death stilled the breath of his irreplaceable Essie.

As he watched Hoser propping pillows under Wilmy's head, a wave of guilt washed over Admah. The boy's failings were his fault. He blamed Hoser when he might have blamed himself.

Or his father, Abner. All those sermons about marital duty and a moral obligation to the bloodline. Those dead babies should have been a warning. Essie had left him in a dark place with Hoser, a son he should try to love.

He could hear Hoser behind the bedroom drape comforting Wilmy. A testy girl at first and resentful of training, Wilmy had come on better than he expected. She made a friend of Hoser, tickling him, and racing around, playing that silly tag game and shouting: "Kings Ex!" when they were breathless for a rest.

Admah studied the sausage splattering in thick grease, listening to the sounds of Wilmy retching, and Hoser talking in hushed tones. After years of marriage, Wilmy made a show of affection for his coon dogs—but not for him. He couldn't complain. Wilmy was never a trial. Her obedience testified to her respect, so the family wouldn't look down on him. And, she had worked wonders with Hoser.

All the beltings in the world couldn't keep Hoser in his grandfather's school. With Wilmy's influence, Hoser could read and do addition and subtraction.

Hoser would do anything for Wilmy. Admah caught their cryptic smiles across the table when they thought he wasn't looking. He didn't mind their laughter. Joy hadn't bothered him in years. It just belonged to other people.

The lugubrious odor of illness hung about the lean-to for months. Neither Wilmy nor Hoser noticed when Admah slipped out to sit at his father Abner's table. At least one of his two wives could be counted on for a good meal.

Wilmy's morning sickness lasted for months. The women brought remedies that were supposed to ease the nausea: honey in warm milk, store-bought soda crackers. Nothing helped.

Laying down the law that she needed to stop malingering didn't help either. Any odor—manure on his boots, his sausage frying, or nutritious cow brains cooked with eggs—dropped Wilmy to the floor in a dead faint.

The town doctor might have helped. Wilmy's daddy warned Admah that he'd take her to the doctor himself if she didn't perk up. The Reaves wouldn't have that. Only their own midwife could handle their women.

By the seventh month, with an odd bump on her stick-limbed body, Wilmy stood up, walked to the kitchen table, and ate a bowl of grits without butter. The phrase "makes me nauseous" left her vocabulary overnight. Hoser cooked whatever appealed to her, rubbed her back, massaged her feet, and propped pillows behind her at every opportunity.

"They's a girl growin' in there," he announced proudly to Admah, as though he were somehow complicit in planting the seed. "I been thinkin' on the name. Wilmy says she thinks Heather is nice or Betty after her ma."

Admah glanced at his son's furrowed brow. "Reaves use names from the Bible for the naming ceremony. Your grandpa preaches on the meaning of the name." Admah stared over Hoser's head into the night, with the faintest sense of uneasiness. "We'd best wait until it gets here before we start naming it."

Estelle had been his Essie's given name, but everyone called her Essie. Admah loved the sound of a name that meant star. His father required a biblical name before he would tie the knot, so Essie told him her biblical name was Esther, so there would be no hitches in the ceremony.

"Hoser, I been thinking on Esther after your ma." He glanced into Wilmy's blatantly astonished face. "If it's no vexation to you, Wilmy."

The vexation of naming her firstborn after her husband's first wife proved no vexation to Wilmy. A foot making an appearance before a head was more than a vexation; it was a misadventure for the mother, the daughter, and the midwife.

After twelve hours of listening to Wilmy's screams and practically hog-tying Hoser to keep him from the birthing room, Admah faced an exhausted midwife.

Her ham-sized hands hung uselessly at her sides when she stepped onto the rough-planed porch outside the lean-to and muttered: "I done the best I know how, Admah. Bottom first I ken handle. But, the laig come out. Then t'other. The haid has a goose egg thin' on top. It's breathin'; that's about all I ken say."

Having been pummeled past endurance and prodded beyond the norm of medical science by a midwife who rarely lost a breech-birthed calf, Wilmy felt nothing but a vast, empty relief that her nightmare of pain had ended.

"It's got lightish hair, Wilmy!" Hoser's voice grated on Wilmy's nerves. The high-pitched cries of the baby girl that repeatedly refused her breast and stiffened with spasms took second place to sleep.

Admah looked across the room at the trio on his bed. Bloody flour sacks had been bundled into a tidy roll and a fresh sheet stretched beneath Wilmy. Her hair spread in limp, damp strands across the pillow. Her closed eyes were festooned with dark circles.

Hoser held the baby awkwardly, poking a bottle of cow's milk at its resisting mouth. A tiny leg stuck out awkwardly from its body, with two small slats of wood taped around it. Hoser adjusted it carefully and looked sternly at his father. "It come out first. Might be broke."

Hoser angled the baby, like a proud parent, toward Admah. "She looks like a Betty. Wilmy don't like old-fashioned names like Esther."

Admah gaped at his new daughter, as if she were an alien. Her ungainly head hung on the stem of her neck like a great, bulbous plant waiting to bloom. This little creature struggling in Hoser's arms would not bloom. Wilmy could name her anything she wanted. It would just be a name left on a stone.

Betty Heather Reave postponed leaving for seven days. When Wilmy woke from her first long sleep, she uncurled tiny, pink fingers, looked into eyes of an indiscriminate hue, and loved her new daughter with a passion she had never known.

Admah moved to a cot in the barn so he wouldn't be troubled by his daughter's constant cries. Hoser made a pallet by Wilmy's bed so he would be handy to walk the floor and rock his new half-sister. He squeezed milk from a clean rag into her mouth and held her little jaws closed, hoping she would not throw it up. She always did.

A week after her torturous journey into the world, Betty Heather slipped quietly into the next. The strangled ululation of Wilmy's screams brought Reaves from every corner of the compound. Abner's two wives wrested the small corpse from Wilmy, leaving Hoser to comfort her.

The Reaves always gathered in a crisis. A demented wife screaming over a dead baby was a doleful sight—even when the baby was marked for death the minute it was born. The women brought greasy chicken broth for Wilmy, who stared at them with great, blank eyes, as though she couldn't remember who they were—or why they were there.

One of Admah's cousins, who had just buried premature twin boys, positioned a small, neatly planed oak casket on the porch. "No need to waste this one. We put the boys together. Plenty of room. They was that little. I saved it for later, but you have need of it."

After the formal sponging of Betty Heather by the midwife, who felt obligated by a bad delivery, the Reave women scurried home to bake cakes, pies, and funeral meats, while Betty settled into her last crib on earth.

Eager to get the baby away from Wilmy's sight so she might get back to normal, Hoser hoisted the casket up with one arm, balanced it on his shoulder, and marched toward the community church as though the third movement of Chopin's Sonata in B-Flat Minor played in a head, where no music had ever played.

Abner waited at the door for his grandson: "Put her on the altar here, Hoser. I put a clean cloth down for the coffin. You go see what you can do for Wilmy. She's plumb distraught. She needs something to lift her spirits, to please her."

Hoser gave Abner a blank look. The mobile of live locusts that he strung together with fishing line above the baby's crib didn't please Wilmy at all. Then, his face lit up. Hoser knew exactly what might please her. The Acme coffee can in the chifferobe brimmed with coins and a few dollar bills. He would take the money to town and buy something real purty for Wilmy to take her mind off her dead baby.

From the portico of the church, Hoser watched the group of men with Admah, moving away from the house over to the corrals. Menfolks steered clear of birthings and funeral fixings. The coast was clear to get the money and to swipe Admah's keys to the old Chevy pickup in the barn. If he left now, he could get into town and be back long before the service that evening.

As the Chevy rattled down the eight miles of dirt roads into Wolfe Flats, Hoser flashed a gap-toothed grin. If he and the cousins had not figured out to hot-wire a car, the Reaves would still be driving mule teams to town. His father claimed that cars left alongside the highway were there for a good reason: engine trouble or out of gas. They belonged to someone.

For once, his Grandfather Abner agreed with Hoser. Abner said the automobiles and pickups were "mislaid" for a reason. If a neighbor's pig wandered into your garden, you butchered him so he couldn't be recognized. A vacated car along the highway, with no one in sight, offered the same possibility.

Abner invested in a generator that could power a sander. Later, he bought tarps, glazing putty, body filler, primer, sealer, and paint. The younger generation of boys needed a vocation to keep them at home.

Now, every Reave family had a pickup with a good engine and rusty fenders. Repainted cars with replaced license plates went to a used car lot in Gainesville, Texas, where nobody asked questions. Once again, the Lord had provided.

CHAPTER TWENTY-THREE

SEEING THINGS

Monday, July 19, 1976

Vernica Roberts sauntered down the main street of Wolfe Flats just as the sun hit its zenith so that the bright light would fall on her head and not slant into eyes, cloudy with cataracts. She might easily stumble on a crack in the sidewalk if the fissures had not been so firmly mapped in her mind. She knew when gaps in the concrete festered; she knew when they split open, just as she knew about everything in Wolfe Flats.

Her gray, shapeless skirt hung limply from her waist, anchored by a strap of leather that had been punctured repeatedly to accommodate her shrinking body. A dark greenish blouse had been hastily tucked into the too-large waistband of the skirt. A shabby cardigan of a dreadful puce color topped her ensemble. A knot of graying hair skewed itself into a no-nonsense coiffure.

The wave of diamonds from a shell-shaped pin, anchoring the edges of her cardigan, flashed in the noonday sun. Round diamonds totalling 146 in number and baguettes tallied at 21, moored into a platinum setting, would defy anyone in Wolfe Flats to define their value.

Dressing well. When appearing in public, one must make a statement in line with decorum. It was the Roberts' way—just as doing minimum upkeep on the exterior of her Victorian house demanded a sizeable annual outlay, though over the years, her grandmother's small art collection had shrunken. Teaching paid for the essentials. It did not repair slate roofs.

Vernica had taught art for thirty years in Wolfe Flats High School, until she was "let go," a phrase that slid easily down the collective gullets of the school board, who dared not question her assertion that she saw angels in trees. William Blake did. So did she, though not so often when she remembered to take those little white pills that the pharmacist at Selvige Drugstore gave her.

Vernica squinted against the bright sunlight at something moving two blocks down the street. From a distance, it looked like one of those old-fashioned perambulators.

She must be seeing things again. No one used those big black baby buggies any longer. Now, women flopped open rickity pastel things with toy-like wheels that buckled dangerously, so the whole apparatus could be scrunched up flat as a pancake. Vernica stepped up her pace and moved a block closer.

A rusted-out pickup driven by a person with no pride idled outside of Selvige's. A man with the chest of an ape was collapsing the perambulator and lifting it into the back of the pickup.

As Vernica watched, he vaulted into the pickup and made an illegal u-turn in the middle of the street; the vehicle whipped a right onto the westbound road and disappeared.

By the time Vernica reached Selvige's, a wraith-like woman had exited the drugstore and begun traveling in frantic circles—from the front of the store over to the diseased elm and back.

Because she suddenly thought of Coleridge, Vernica started to say: "Weave a circle round him thrice/ and close your eyes with holy dread" until she saw the young woman brace and cram her fist into a mouth that screamed silently.

When the woman saw Vernica watching her, a strange language erupted from her. *Slavic* thought Vernica, but with a choked sound as though the woman did not want the words to have life.

"My baby. I left her here while I used the telephone inside. Someone stole my baby!" The accusation in the woman's heavily accented English riled Vernica for a moment.

"People in Wolfe Flats do not steal babies," Vernica retorted with more confidence than she was feeling. "I did see a pickup here with a man loading something in the back of it."

"Milo! Milo!" screamed the woman, who suddenly looked very young and absolutely terrified.

She clutched Vernica's arm with such ferocity that Vernica found herself plastered face-to-face with Picasso's Weeping Woman.

The girl's shoulder-length hair, formerly the color of ripe wheat, hung in strands of drab purple and acidic lemon; her ice-blue eyes turned black as lumps of coal; tears rolled like nodules of frozen pain down her cheeks; her flushed face took on a greenish cast.

"What's going on out here? Is she bothering you, Miss Roberts?" the irritated voice of Selvige's owner, Peregrine Hamm, intervened.

"This young woman says that her baby has been stolen in front of your store." Vernica looked askance at the narrow glass door fronting the drugstore, a troublesome door that she always struggled to pry open.

"She probably couldn't get her perambulator in that stingy opening you call an entrance."

Vernica eyed Peregrine as he sorted out the news of a stolen baby and the complaints about his front door. His squat, obese body gave off a faint sour odor. A network of purplish spider veins spread from his cheeks up to a receding hairline. They might be sending a message to his brain, but Vernica didn't think so.

"This foreign woman came in demanding to use my business phone. I even looked up the Posey's number so she could call. No one answered, but she kept dialing and dialing. She didn't say she had a baby with her."

Peregrine frowned at the sobbing woman and flapped his plump hands up and down, exposing unpleasant sockets of dampness around his armpits. "What kind of woman would leave her baby outside in this heat? She might have another agenda—calling the Posey number like that, I mean."

Vernica touched the thin back of the girl, who bent over with great, retching sobs, looking more like Picasso's "suffering machine" than any canvas could capture.

"Agenda!" The tone of Vernica's voice sent a fresh blast of purple through Peregrine's troubled veins.

"If this girl says someone took her baby, then someone did. Go inside and call Sheriff Bemis. Tell him to come immediately!" Watching Peregrine move one fat flank against the door and struggle to hold it open while the heavy glass door fought for closure, Vernica felt a tinge of regret that Peregrine's mother had read Smollett and named her only son for a character's despised son—Peregrine Pickle.

∽

Corpulent, jowly, and furious that Peregrine's phone call had interrupted his foray into chicken fried steak, smoggy with gravy, Sheriff Orville Bemis arrived and dismissed the sidewalk gawkers as decisively as Caesar crossed the Rubicon.

Under the direct sun, the face that Orville turned toward Vernica had the texture and color of a skinned rabbit. "I know what you think you saw, Miz Roberts, but your eyes ain't what they used to be when you was teaching."

The Sheriff's dismissal of her was a two-pronged insult: her artist eyes were no longer trustworthy, and everyone would be reminded that she had lost her teaching job.

"You, young woman. Quit yelling. Speak English! You get on down to my office. Talk to Deputy Helms. He'll take a statement. Yes, yes, you can tell him to call Mr. Posey but Peregrine here says no one answered when you called. Just tell my deputy. He'll get it all down."

He turned to Peregrine and whispered just loudly enough to be overheard, while he watched Vernica Roberts lead the still-sobbing woman toward the courthouse: "Lord. What will that woman come up with next? A big man who resembles a devil put a buggy in his pickup. A month ago she was seeing thousands of angels in a tree."

He rubbed his bulging stomach thoughtfully, as he watched Vernica steer the woman across the street toward the courthouse. "Nice ass on that foreign woman. My dinner's cold by now, I reckon. Wonder why she was calling the Posey house? Not worth following up on." Sheriff Bemis' conclusion was almost as apt as Caesar's "*alea iacta est*" (the die is cast) as he crossed the Rubicon.

Lacking the imagination to know that an infinity of angels could roost in a tree since they do not occupy space, Sheriff Bemis accepted only two premises about the hubbub that interrupted his meal: one, people with foreign accents are naturally suspect; and two, citizens of Wolfe County do not snatch babies off Main Street in broad daylight. The birthrate in Wolfe County outstripped all other statistics. Children were not in short supply.

CHAPTER TWENTY-FOUR

EVENING IN PARIS

Noon, Monday, July 19, 1976

A nd the Lord provided again. When Hoser rattled into town around the middle of the day
that same Monday and parked along the curb by
Selvige's Drugstore, the focus of his attention was
on the blue crystal vials of Evening in Paris that
lined the glass case just inside the door.

When Hoser and Wilmy could talk Admah into
the rare treat of a town visit, they would always head
to the front window of Selvige's Drugstore. "I could
stand there admiring them perfume bottles forever
when Daddy took me inside for a fountain Coke.
They was too pricey. I smelt one onct. Like heaven."
Wilmy's eyes would glaze over with a dull expression,

as though heaven would never be accessible inside cobalt glass.

Hoser hefted the coffee can of coins. He should have counted the money before he left. He'd do it now. He made neat little piles of quarters, dimes, and nickels on the flat plane of the pickup seat, adding in his head as he stacked them; he bent over to swoop them back into the can.

The mewling sound of Betty Heather caused him to sit up so quickly that he cracked his head on the gearshift. Right outside the pickup window, careening down the sidewalk, was a large, awkwardly shaped buggy with some kind of folding suspension system under it.

He gaped at the willowy blond woman pushing the buggy. She looked like one of those expensive town women, but different. The nervous, edgy way she kept looking behind her reminded him of a rabbit just before the dogs get it. She rammed the buggy into the door at Selvige's, pushing and pushing. She'd never get that thing through the narrow, glass-fronted door.

She pulled it back, leaned across it, made soft noises, and shook the buggy gently. The crying stopped. She pulled the hood of the buggy down, pushed it under the half-diseased elm by the sidewalk outside of Selvige's, set the brake and hurried into the store.

Hoser eased out of the pickup, leaving the door ajar. A block down the sidewalk, he could see an old woman meandering along, looking in store windows. Not another soul was on the street. The courthouse clock struck twelve chimes. It was noon. That's when town folks had their dinner. He walked swiftly over to the buggy, flipped back the top and gasped.

Betty Heather stared up at him with eyes so blue you could drown in them. Below a puff of hair as pale as taffy, fat pink cheeks invited touch. He did, and tiny fingers raked his hand. It was a sign.

In less than a minute, Hoser squashed down the buggy with the baby inside and hoisted the contraption into the bed of the pickup. Two minutes later, his Chevy had cleared the main street of town and made it to the crossroads of the railroad track where a back road led to the West End.

A half-filled bottle of milk and a pacifier settled Wilmy's new baby, as Hoser tiptoed into the church before sundown. He had parked near a grove of soapberry trees just off the road and hotfooted it into the compound. The women would be finishing the milking in the barn just about now. He'd move the pickup into the barn later.

Abner's service would start after sundown, when the chores were done. Someone would have already dug a little hole, because of unseasonable heat. Hot weather hastened funerals. Abner said the odor of decay made for bad memories of a loved one.

Hoser placed the new Betty against the plinth of the altar so she couldn't roll off the slightly raised platform where his grandfather preached.

He gently pushed aside the lid of the coffin and squinted down at the yellowing, shrunken baby. Someone had hidden its goose egg with a knitted cap and wrapped the baby in a crocheted blanket. Not a new one. He rolled the body tightly into the blanket and held it up. Light as a feather. He wondered how such a little thing could make such a big bump on Wilmy and cause her such pain with the getting here.

CHAPTER TWENTY-FIVE

A MIRACLE

The miracle revealed itself to Abner first. Just before he rang the bell to summon his clan to the service, Abner visited the community room, lifting lids, sampling a fried chicken leg, and tracing a skinny finger along the bottom edge of a chocolate frosted cake, so no one would notice.

A baby's cry was an expected sound in Abner's church. A wobbling coffin was not. Abner crept closer to the altar. Beneath the slightly ajar coffin lid, something moved. Rats more than likely. Already at his granddaughter. Abner seized a bronze candlestick off the altar and shoved the casket lid off.

A blonde, blue-eyed cherub stared up at him. With his shout of "Hallelujah!" echoing through the church, Abner dashed to the portico and yanked the bell clapper with the force of half a dozen ringers sounding out joy and alarm at the same time.

By the time that Hoser had put away the shovel and dumped the perambulator in a sinkhole on the south forty, the entire Reave clan had assembled on its collective knees. Tears, rejoicing, the laying on of hands in forbidden places, and general mayhem was in force on pews and under pews.

As soon as Wilmy staggered in on weak legs, held upright by Abner's wives, Abner placed the Lazarus baby in her arms and shouted: "Enough! Take your places! Praise must proceed before celebration."

He then launched into the best extemporaneous sermon of his career, telling his flock about Elijah the Tishbite who took the last cake of meal from a starving widow and her son. Fated to eat only twigs of wood with his mother, the baby died; then, Elijah shouted: "O Lord, let this child's soul come into him again!"

Raising his arms upward, Abner's voice soared, "The widow's son stirred, and she shouted to Elijah: 'The word of the Lord in thy mouth is truth.'" Abner's white hair shimmered under the swinging kerosene lantern above: the clan's own prophet with his own miracle.

Admah pushed his way through a throng of cousins and second cousins, with men clapping him on the back and women hugging him in an unconventional display of emotion. Public affection nettled Admah.

He propped himself against the back wall of the room and stared at the quartet in front of the altar. Admah had an innate ability to separate wheat from chaff; he needed to shuck off this uneasy feeling.

His pa would seize any opportunity to align himself with a biblical prophet. That's how he had kept the clan under his thumb all these years: squeezing out devils that no one could see; encouraging the hysterical to babble in tongues; copping a quick feel from a distraught female parishioner.

He watched his wife, squatting by the altar, holding a pink and white baby with no knobs on its head. Wilmy's expression could only be described as beatific.

Hoser bent over her, his stubby shoulders flexed, as though wings might sprout at any moment. He grabbed the infant and held it aloft to a cheering and sobbing clan.

Hoser resembled a grotesque version of Gabriel, who had come to deliver the good news, but decided to outstay his welcome.

As Hoser seized the baby again, Admah saw the naked look of fear on Wilmy's face. It settled into her eyes, as Hoser reluctantly handed the baby back. Admah gave Hoser the once over.

His son had been up to something this afternoon. Admah's photographic memory clicked into gear. The Chevy was parked in the barn just off center. *Everything* tonight was just off center.

Admah narrowed his eyes at Hoser, who was exhibiting himself at the altar like he was the miracle maker. It was time for Wilmy to tend the baby and Hoser to get back to the field. Boys his age shouldn't have such an unnatural interest in babies.

Early in the morning, he would send Hoser to check on the fence in the wheat pasture, next to Hickory Creek, to see if rising water had washed out any posts.

At seven o'clock the next morning, Hoser pummeled the sides of the mule heartlessly, forcing it faster and faster down the deer trail that led to the far north end of the wheat pasture. He could see the arch of the old train bridge that no one used any longer. Just this side of the bridge, a hard-packed gravel road split east and west along Hickory Creek.

"Whoa. Hold up there." Hoser reined in the mule and slid noiselessly off his back, looping the reins around the stump of a Hackberry. Weaving through a cluster of redbuds tucked into the corner of the pasture, Hoser inched nearer the boundary road.

With the keys dangling in the ignition, a shiny, black Pontiac Firebird sat touting its 350 V-8 engine and Turbo 350 transmission.

Hoser crawled under a strand of barbed wire and crouched beside the car. Just beyond the road by a steep slope dropping into Hickory Creek, the sound of a fist making contact with a body was music to his ears. If the owner of the Firebird was distracted—either hitting or being hit—maybe he could make off with the car.

A lightning-struck hedge apple tree provided a perfect view through its ragged fork. A man with coal-black hair, so shiny it might have been smeared with engine oil, delivered blow after blow to a woman who moaned softly, a small, frightened animal too afraid to bolt.

Like an enraged gorilla, the man's face twisted in fury as he aimed blows to her ribs, her kidneys, and her breasts, carefully avoiding her face. This man had mastered the art of doing maximum damage in places where it wouldn't show.

His harsh words sounded like gibberish to Hoser. He couldn't understand a thing he was demanding of the woman. Whatever it was, she wasn't answering.

Hoser squatted down like a misshapen toad, perfectly still, until he felt a familiar throb between his legs. It had been coming on for more than a year, especially when he indulged in a secret pleasure of torturing weak critters. Lately, it came on at odd times—when he sat close to Wilmy or watched her fiddling with her sick baby.

The woman's fingers, scrabbling for a hold in the gravel embankment, triggered a cascade of pebbles into the creek below. As she slid backward, Hoser got a clear view of her face. It was the woman with the buggy on the sidewalk outside Selvige's.

Now, standing with the woman just above the pylon of the bridge, with the creek flashing in the morning light behind them, the man might have been her lover, tenderly holding her against his chest.

Continuing to hold her, he pivoted her away from him, caressed the sides of her face with both hands, rolled his fat thumbs just above the delicate hyoid, and splintered her life away with a single thrust.

Hoser gasped and clamped a hand over his mouth. In her destruction, she took on a terrible beauty, her cheeks as flushed as late apples, her eyes so achingly blue, like a summer sky that defies the naming of its color.

Flinging the door open, Hoser plopped down in the driver's seat, slammed the car into reverse, and backed down the gravel road. Within seconds, the gorilla appeared in the road, bigger than King Kong on the Giant Classic comic book cover that Wilmy had bought to help him read. This gorilla wasn't perched on a building and snatching up airplanes. This one was racing down the road toward him and gaining.

An eight-cylinder engine makes a comforting sound when it meets up with something less durable than a muscle car with Uniroyal steel-belted tires. Hoser didn't give it a second thought as he made the second pass over the gorilla, a third pass, and then stopped the Firebird to see if the hump on the gravel road moved.

It didn't. Hoser heaved it into the trunk, scuffed his boot against the place in the gravel where road kill bled, and took a dirt road along a remote stretch of the creek where nothing but wild pigs traveled. He could strip this fancy car so that no one could recognize it. The pigs would do the same for the man.

CHAPTER TWENTY-SIX

A FLOATER

Tuesday, July 20, 1976

When Bubba Simpson and his cousin Junior Wilson burst into the Sheriff's office just before noon on Tuesday, they joustled each other like contestants at a sack race, shouting: "I saw her first. I'll tell."

They had been telling all the way from where they parked illegally to the courthouse door, attracting stragglers along the way.

"We was hopin' to snag somethin' on a trot line when we come round the bend, just where the creek's been gettin' out of the bank by the old bridge; we seen somethin' curious, the yaller hair floatin' out. Give us the creeps. Sent chills down my spine in spite of the heat." Junior had an annoying habit of drawing out a story with his own reactions for dramatic effect.

Bubba came right to the point. "A woman's hooked by one of them concrete pillars under the old bridge, dead as a doornail." Bubba nodded companionably toward Orville Bemis. When the sheriff decided to replace his deputy, Bubba wanted to be first in line. "We didn't touch her body, Sheriff. Your business 'n all."

At that very moment, Deputy Helms, who was on the phone when the boys burst into the office, made it someone else's business.

The young woman that Vernica Roberts had brought into his office yesterday haunted his dreams last night. After describing her baby and the perambulator, she refused to give anything but her name— Eve Jones. He was sure that wasn't her name.

When Vernica interrupted the woman with, "You shouted out 'Milo.' Is that your baby's name?" The look of hatred that the young woman turned on her stunned both Vernica and the deputy.

"Is no name. Is the devil," she snarled.

"That's *exactly* the description of the man I saw putting that perambulator in his pickup. I told Orville, but he dismissed me as a half-blind, half-wit nuisance. It's amazing to me that someone who could draw a rabbit in the style of Durer would work for a man like Orville Bemis. You disappoint me, Willie." She watched Willie Helms shuffling his papers uneasily. He had been a boy who never wanted to disappoint. Neither did Eliot Posey, she remembered, though he often did.

She got back on track. "Peregrine Hamm said that this young woman was using his telephone to call the Posey house. No one answered, but she tried over and over. I think they took Lilymae to the City for her appointment with that nerve doctor," she whispered to Deputy Helms, casting her eyes down, as though revealing a family secret.

Vernica stared at the girl who had stiffened like Lot's wife, as though someone had forgotten to warn her not to look upon Sodom and Gomorrah. "I don't know if she knows the Poseys. I asked, but she won't say."

"I will come back later to see if you have found my baby." The hollow tone of the young woman's voice sounded like the final, muffled knell of a church bell. "No. I will sign no papers." She shoved aside the deputy's pen and turned toward the door. Her wide, dry, Winsor-blue eyes were fixed on something unnameable that only she could see. She brushed past Vernica without a backward glance.

Stunned into silence, Vernica thought about the mythological goddess Niobe whose hubris cost her the lives of her fourteen children and turned her into an eternally weeping stone. *This young woman had moved past tears to boundless terror.*

∽

"I don't know what you two think you seen, but if you messed up a perfectly good crime scene, you ain't heard the last from me. Get on out to your car and wait. I'll lead the way directly," Sheriff Bemis struggled to shove his heel into an ill-fitting new boot wedged at an angle by his chair. "If you can get off the phone long enough to help, Willie, you might want to call the ambulance service in Ardmore. Just in case we got more 'an a drowned cow here. Take your own vehicle out to the bridge. I got things to do after we sort this."

Within fifteen minutes, Sheriff Bemis's Cutless Supreme whipped out of the side parking lot, followed by Willie's old Ford truck. Bubba's short-bed pickup cut across a bed of zinneas, leaped the curb, and swerved in front of the deputy's truck at the cross streets of Main and Cherokee. Bubba and Junior needed to be hot on the Sheriff's heels to explain away any "irregularities" at the crime scene. A free-floating jugline wasn't exactly a trotline.

After five miles on Highway 77, the trio of vehicles slowed down to a crawl to avoid axle-breaking potholes on the stretch of a gravel road leading east to the old Hickory Creek Bridge.

Eliot Posey's Commodore appeared out of nowhere and swerved onto the gravel road just ahead of the sheriff, paying no heed to Orville's sudden flashing lights and siren. Angling his tires onto the grass verge, Eliot raced along the road and jolted to a stop alongside a great hulk of twisting metal that hunkered over Hickory Creek, now flooding bank to bank with a summer rainstorm.

Flinging open the door of his car, Eliot ran toward a crumbling substructure of concrete pillars, partially submerged by high water. Sheriff Bemis stumbled behind him, shouting: "Possible crime scene, Eliot! Law enforcement only! Step aside!"

Both of the men stopped just at the point where the gravel embankment slanted toward the creek. The muddy water effervesced around truncated pylons, holding up one end of the iron skeleton of a bridge. Below them, a single shoe aimlessly lifted and fell like a lost fishing cork.

"This here's the wrong angle, Sheriff. We could see her plain as day from the boat," Bubba edged closer, as Junior elbowed his way into the group and stared down at the debris from washed-out fields. "The creek rose so fast; they's too much trash caught up here," Bubba said.

"Exactly! You and Junior get the hell back from here until you're called." Sheriff Bemis could hear the remote sound of the ambulance tearing down the highway. He cocked his ear toward the sound and grinned as it became fainter.

"Bubba, you get out on the highway and wave down the ambulance. I told them third gravel road to the west. Makes no nevermind if we don't find nothin' for them. They can't follow directions worth a damn."

Neither could Eliot Posey. Orville Bemis watched as Eliot skidded down the bank, stepped on top of a raft-like mass of willow branches lodged next to the pylon, plunged waist-deep into the water, and pulled the body of a woman against him.

Her pale blond hair wafted behind her like feathers on an exotic fishing lure. Only the tissue around her open eyes showed signs of maceration. Her face and neck and hands were white, wrinkled like fine linen.

With a fearsome intensity, Eliot clutched the body to him, staggering against the rushing water, and murmuring: "Mirna, Mirna, Mirna," as though he could will her to stand with him in the fast-moving creek.

"I'll take her now, Eliot." The firm voice of Willie Helms made Eliot release his hold and let the body drift against the deputy who eased it up onto the gravel bank.

Sheriff Bemis stood well back from the action. He could hear the crunch of gravel from the ambulance coming down the road. Fishing bloated bodies out of creeks was a job for deputies or techs.

Having Eliot Posey show up like this and recognize the drowned woman could complicate things. The fact that he had been in the same high school class with Eliot's sister meant nothing to an arrogant Posey. Eliot showed no respect for his office. So, nothing was owed to him.

Sheriff Bemis glared down at his deputy, fiddling with the body, pulling off debris, arranging the arms too carefully. Willie complicated things, such as taking down every word of a hysterical foreigner yesterday.

If that woman hadn't made such a fuss about some non-existent baby and if Peregrine Hamm hadn't told Miz Roberts the woman was using his phone to call the Posey house, the thing could be easily tied up as a drug-related crime.

With no bullet holes or stab wounds in plain sight, just the mention of cocaine or LSD was usually Orville's go-to method for solving unexplained deaths of strangers in Wolfe County. With the state line just a few miles south, Texas was ripe for blame— and this woman did get off the Greyhound bus from Ft. Worth.

Orville's jumbled thoughts hit a roadblock. Even if the drug angle worked for this foreign woman, her phone call to the Poseys threw up a roadblock. Poseys wouldn't associate with users.

Inching toward the soggy corpse, Orville peered down at a shell-like ear, pale as the nacre inside a nautilus. "She's a druggie. Look at all them earrings from one end of her ear to t'other."

"Not an earring, Sheriff. Those are fishhooks that snagged her. Somebody's trotline got her caught up in these bridge pilings."

Orville's deputy flashed a sympathetic glance toward Eliot. Knowing that he had probably just ended his career as a deputy, he might as well compound his felony. "When this woman came into the office, I don't think she was on drugs. She was frightened of someone and desperate to find her baby."

"There wasn't no baby! Just like I told you yesterday. Some of us know how to do our jobs, Willie." Sheriff Bemis lifted a single, scornful eyebrow at his disgraced deputy.

"I found a witness who saw her get off the Greyhound around noon. She was carrying a big bag, not a baby. I expect she was trying to call her dealer on Peregine's phone. She *was* hallucinating when I talked to her outside the drugstore. I've seen dozens of addicts in that state. I'll have no more out of you, *Mister* Helms." Sheriff Bemis stressed the "mister" to make it clear that no official termination would be necessary.

The rattling of a gurney at the top of the embankment reminded Orville who was in charge. He shouted up to the two volunteers: "Them damn boys tromped all over this place; you might as well take her."

Orville picked his way along the boggy bank to where an ashen Eliot Posey stood, his hand braced against Willie's shoulder for support.

Deputies had no business cozying up to people like the Poseys, especially in an election year. The image of Willie Helms and Annabel Posey snuggling up on the dance floor at their high school graduation party surfaced like acid reflux. It was a night that still pained Orville to remember.

After being loaded with Sue Ann into the principal's car, under the watchful eyes of thirty classmates, Orville would never forget the humiliation of that night—or the thirty frozen faces motionless as a color guard outside the Posey mansion.

Orville rearranged his face carefully. As the duly elected head of law enforcement, it was time to demonstrate the law's caring side, but with his own characteristic firmness. "This accidental drowning here, Eliot. It's for law enforcement to handle. Doc Blake will take a look at the body. You need to go on about your business. There's nothing more you can do here."

There was. The sharp crack of a body bag zipper announced the splash of projectile vomit now spreading over the sheriff's new Tony Lama boots.

When Eliot Posey stopped gagging, his snooty Posey voice carried a threat that Orville dared not ignore: "Orville, that quack is not to touch her."

He turned to the tech, quietly easing the zipper along the body bag. "Take her to the medical examiner in Ardmore. Tell him I'll be calling him." Eliot turned toward the deputy. "Can you come over to my car, Willie? We need to talk."

CHAPTER TWENTY-SEVEN

NO CRIME

Sheriff Bemis scuffed the toes of his boots in the wet sandbank and squinted past Eliot at his deputy. Ex-deputy. Eliot had arrived at the crime scene too quickly. Leaking information was a breach of loyalty. Loyalty to the sheriff was the only criterion for longevity in Wolfe County law enforcement. Deputy Helms had just failed his annual performance evaluation when he stepped across the boundary.

Time to set another boundary. "My deputy answers to no one but me, Eliot. He'll be answering soon enough," he glowered at Willie. "If you've got information about this corpse here, you'd better tell it to me."

With a face that flamed from ashen to a furious red, Eliot whirled toward the sheriff. Orville shifted his boots backward. "The reason I will not talk to you, Orville, is that you don't know how to listen."

Eliott flicked his finger against Orville's badge. "The woman in that . . . that . . ." his voice faltered, as though he could not name the zippered bag.

"Yesterday, this woman asked you to help find her baby, and you dismissed her as a nuisance. Vernica Roberts phoned me this morning . . . about a woman who tried to call me from Selvige's yesterday. This woman." He pointed toward the body bag on the gurney where the ambulance driver stood, uneasy about which orders to follow. It was Sheriff Beamis's case, but this was Posey's county.

"After Vernica phoned me, I called Willie; I could hear everything those boys said in your office. I drove here to check it out myself. Don't blame Willie for doing his job. He tried to get more information yesterday, but he said she clammed up and left."

"Well, that's it!" Orville brushed Eliot's arm familiarly. "That's what people on the wrong side of the law do. They clam up."

He nodded dismissively at his deputy. "Despite what Deputy Helms may have told you, I do my job. I personally took the time to investigate this woman's complaint. I ascertained that she came in on the Greyhound bus around noon yesterday. I have one witness who saw her get off at the bus stop. She didn't have a baby with her."

"What witness, Orville?" The ice in Eliot's voice would have frozen a lesser man.

Contentiousness was not called for. "Tom Coonce. Hanging around the bus depot, and he was stone-cold sober when I talked to him."

Eliot Posey gaped at the sheriff. Orville stared back, processing his case by the book. Law enforcement professionals should engage in a detailed investigation of the facts. These being hard to come by, they should probe the omissions in a case and let intuition guide them.

For Sheriff Bemis, when intuition failed, bias stepped right up to the plate. He wouldn't want to tip the delicate balance of the scales of justice in the face of a sure thing.

His summary of the death of the woman under the old Hickory Creek bridge was a model of clarity: "Drug addict. She had a meltdown in front of Selvige's about an imaginary baby. Peregrine Hamm was a witness to her hallucinations. Vernica Roberts can attest that the woman refused to cooperate with my deputy. She wandered off in a delusional state. With this morning's findings, I now deduce that she probably fell through rotten slats on the bridge and drowned. The coroner will agree."

Like a coven of militants, Eliot, the sheriff, and the ex-deputy bristled at each other as they formed a semi-circle by the gurney, staring down at the body bag as though a macerated face, already white and dimpled as a plucked goose, might pop open the zipper to disagree with the coroner.

"Vernica Roberts wouldn't agree," Eliot's imperious voice sliced through the tension. "She saw a perambulator. She saw someone put it in the back of a pickup. She told you," the accusation in Eliot's voice gave Orville cause to tone down his retort.

"Come on, Eliot. We're talking loony tunes. The school board had to put Miz Roberts out to pasture. When she gets off her pills, she sees angels in trees. Angels, for crying out loud. In broad daylight." Sheriff Bemis's wheedling tone might invite a lesser man into his confidence.

Chary of such blatant skepticism, Eliot snapped back, "So did William Blake. See angels in broad daylight. He didn't see a baby buggy being loaded into a pickup. That fact alone should have made you listen to her."

"I did listen. I sent Miz Roberts with the foreign woman to give a report to my deputy, but you heard him say she wasn't cooperative. We have a statement from Peregrine Hamm. It's hard to get statements from angels." Orville shot a conspiratorial grin in the direction of the ambulance crew, who eased the gurney toward the back of the ambulance with stony faces.

"She goes to the ME in Ardmore, Orville. You'd better get your worthless ass out there looking for the pickup Vernica Roberts saw in front Selvige's at noon yesterday. Put out an alert for a missing baby!"

Glancing down at the drying puke on his boots, Orville watched Eliot Posey heading to his car, without so much as a backward glance at the lawman who had just begun to think about what kind of job that might lie ahead of him since that worthless deputy of his was history. Did Eliot know how many pickups were in Wolfe County?

The sheriff frowned at the back of his deputy trailing behind Posey. He would keep Willie around long enough to find out why Eliot was taking such an interest in a drowned woman. Annabel Posey might know. She always had the look of knowing more than she let on—even in high school.

Those half-filled filing cabinets that cluttered his brain suddenly popped ajar. Over twenty-five years ago, as he strutted on stage to snap up the Athlete of the Year trophy on graduation day, Orville could remember only perfunctory applause. The heartfelt cheers came for Willie Helms as valedictorian with a scholarship to Oklahoma A&M.

That stuck-up Annabel Posey was hot on Willie's heels as salutatorian. In their four years as classmates, Orville couldn't remember a single instance of Annabel being rude, but the scent of entitlement that hung about in the very air that she breathed rankled.

Orville sucked in his gut as he watched the ambulance maneuvering along the gravel road to turn north on Highway 77 back to Ardmore. Remembering that stupid graduation party at Annabel's still set his teeth on edge. The hired band from Ardmore had just launched into "Mona Lisa" when he and Sue Ann Coonce neared the edge of the circus-sized tent spread across the Posey side yard.

Bringing an older girl with oversized tits to the party might have been a mistake, especially since she couldn't keep her choc beer down or her underwear up. As his daddy put it, Sue Ann was in season. The gash of her smirk flashed toward the pack of single boys huddled in a cluster by the dance floor.

"You're so like that lady with the mystic smile," an untrained baritone groaned into the mic just as Willie spun Annabel across the pre-fab dance floor in front of Orville.

There he was, the star athlete at Wolfe Flats High, condescending to take a whirl with the hostess, even though Annabel was plain as an old shoe. There was no doubt that Annabel knew Orville had made a late entrance. Girls like her always sent certain signals with their eyes to guys like him. Hopeful eyes. Came with the territory.

Under the yellow bug lights, the frothy pink concoction swathing Annabel reflected an ethereal aura about her, so that Orville saw a smile as mysterious as the Mona Lisa's—sent in his direction.

With the forcefulness that only a four-sport letterman could muster, Orville shot an arm out to catch the twirling Annabel and came up with only a fragment of pink taffeta in his hand. Annabel didn't scream. Sue Ann did. "Hoo, boy! You have *ex*-posed the hostess." Her peals of laughter rang out above shocked silence.

Orville's muffled excuses and Annabel's stricken face did nothing to deter the principal from packing him and Sue Ann into his car and driving them home to the tune of threats about "public drunkenness" and "withholding his diploma."

As Orville thought back to that time, the celebrations on the high school stage hadn't served Willie or Annabel—or him. College football never was an option for a poor boy with more bluffs than touchdowns.

That clever Willie didn't make it through his first semester at A&M before his folks' car skidded on ice across 77 into a stalled hay truck. With three younger brothers at home, Willie got to grow old before his time.

Orville smiled disparagingly. A deputy's pay couldn't make much of a dent in a mortgaged farm. So much for valedictorians and people getting above themselves.

Annabel had gone away to college, only as far as Durant, but she came back home—just like Eliot, who had stayed away in Boston as long as he could.

That old vampire of a mother kept an unholy grip on both her kids. Orville grunted as he cranked his car into action. He could almost pity Annabel and Eliot if the Poseys didn't own half the county and most of the commissioners. He still had the law on his side during an investigation. It would be what he said it was.

But it wasn't. The ME in Ardmore failed to confirm a single one of Sheriff Bemis' hypotheses. No drugs were found in the woman's system. She had recently given birth. The disc-shaped bruises along the jaw-line and a broken hyoid indicated strangulation leading to sudden vagal cardiac arrest. Immersion in water occurred after death.

It was time to search for a baby that may or may not have been with the victim on the Greyhound bus. It was also time to search for a murderer, but Orville had no idea where to start.

"Start with a man called Milo." Vernica Roberts collared the sheriff as he was sneaking out the back door of the courthouse, away from the ME's report on his desk. "That's the name that poor girl shouted when I told her I had seen a man loading something in the back of his pickup. I told Eliot what she said, and I'm sure he recognized that name."

Orville swatted Vernica's hand away. "My deputy has taken down all the information Eliot has about the victim. You need to go check on your angels, Miz Roberts, and let me do my job. Yout interference is disrupting the advancement of my progress in this case."

Vernica watched Sheriff Bemis get into an impressive Oldsmobile, neatly stenciled with "Wolfe County Sheriff" on the door and peal out of the parking lot. Orville Bemis eased perks like personal vehicles and gas allotments and per diems into his own coffer.

She doubted that he had done much more today than he had the day before. Solving a puzzling crime would be such a big idea that Orville would have trouble holding on to it. He would categorically define the dead woman as a nuisance and a missing baby that no one had seen as just a phantom.

CHAPTER TWENTY-EIGHT

A VISIT

Wednesday, July 21, 1976

I t had been almost twenty-five years since Willie Helms had knocked at her door.

Standing this close, Annabel felt an impulse to fold him in a narcissistic embrace, as though she were experiencing her own past return and was strangely moved by it.

She had been watching the boy disappear for years, but the man standing at her door startled her. Deep lines splayed out from eyes more topaz than hazel. The ill-fitting regulation polyester shirt pilled around the collar. His large brown hands hung uselessly at his sides. He shuffled his boots on the front mat, as though the soles wouldn't come clean.

"Sorry to trouble you, Annabel. I'm here on the Sheriff's business. About that woman," he added reluctantly.

She felt an uncomfortable curiosity about why Willie was standing on her porch—the same belated curiosity one feels when passing the aftermath of a car wreck, the same sense of dreadful relief that all the bloodied parts have been tidied up and put away.

"It's about Eliot knowing the woman who died down by the bridge. The Sheriff wonders if you knew her." A deep flush rose from his collar to the roots of his graying hair, a testament to his humiliation for asking such a weighted question.

Like Buridan's ass between two bales of hay, Annabel could have decided on an answer. She might blurt out her mother's suspicions that Eliot was seeing a woman in Ft. Worth several months ago—all those mysterious trips that he made, with her mother checking the odometer. Not asking, just prying.

Or, Annabel could have told Willie about Vernica Roberts's phone call the previous night about someone connected to the dead woman, about a man named Milo that Eliot intended to kill.

Willie filled in the uncomfortable gap. "Eliot knew her. He told me she was pregnant and went into hiding six months ago. He said he gave up trying to find her for fear of leading a man called Milo to her. Your brother won't tell me anything else. I think they had a relationship. There's nothing Orville would like better than to charge him," Willie blurted out.

"What crime, Deputy Helms? Fornication? But that was in another country, and besides the wench is dead." The *Jew of Malta* popping into her head startled Annabel, as did her unexpectedly harsh response.

She knew everything that everyone in Wolfe Flats knew: a young woman was killed by Hickory Bridge; the same young woman claimed that her baby had been stolen outside of Selvige's drugstore; the next day, Eliot had arrived at the crime scene at the same time that the sheriff and his deputy got there; and, Eliot had interfered with the sheriff's business.

After Vernica's call, Annabel knew more than she wanted to know. The fact that Eliot wanted to kill someone named Milo spoke to her brother's passion for this dead woman. Eliot always controlled his impulses.

"If you can help your brother, I know you will. You know where to find me." Willie moved with purposeful strides off the porch.

Annabel stared wordlessly, as Willie headed toward his pickup. From this distance, he looked almost like the lanky boy with whom she had shared a brief infatuation.

She watched him drive away, his arm moving out the window, his hand waving back in a gesture that was something like a salute, warm and intimate, exactly like that night of their graduation party. Here on the porch, watching his truck travel down the gravel road, she could almost feel herself moving apart from him, into middle age, her flesh drooping, her blood growing cold. Settling in with King Rich-ard for a long "winter of our discontent."

For years, there had not been much to reconcile her to growing old, just a vague memory of metal ridges in a pickup bed and Willie lying the length of her, no weight at all.

The weight came from worrying about why Eliot had missed his life. About a year ago, he seemed to have found one. At that time, his secretiveness had troubled her and turned their mother into a specu-lative bore. "I told you it was Ft. Worth, Annabel. The odometer reads 180 on the nose. Same as three days ago. Same as a week ago. Your brother has found someone of interest."

"Or a new bookstore. Or a new CPA. Or a new lawyer. Eliot makes trips out of town on business, always has." Annabel tried to shift her mother away from the scent, covering for Eliot as usual.

"He makes *those* kinds of trips to Oklahoma City. That's 230 miles, not 180. He tells me when he leaves on business. This is different. You need to find out about the woman he's seeing. She might not be right for our family. We still have hope for Eliot. You're long past any pipe dreams."

Annabel might have snarled in response had her mother's pale face not looked so much like the aging Queen Elizabeth, her face glistening damply under the sheen of thick powder.

Usually, it was Eliot's ambivalence to his charmed life that wore Annabel down: clever, handsome Eliot tiptoeing across a world at his feet without giving it a second glance. Now, it was her mother, reaffirming Annabel's disappointment, as though she were born to it. She smiled at her mother's use of "pipe dreams." Opium might soften the rasp of her mother's tongue.

That evening, after Willie's visit to question her, Annabel watched Eliot brooding on the porch swing. He had ignored their mother's pointed comments during dinner. "I had two calls today from ladies in my bridge group about that drowned woman. They said her baby might have floated all the way to Mexico by now. She was foreign."

The quizzical face that turned toward her frozen-eyed children was greedy for information. "I can't rely on my own children for important news," she added, peevishly.

"Viking I landed on Mars today, Mother, and is digging up dirt as we speak. Not that much different from some of your bridge friends," Annabel couldn't keep the sarcasim out of her voice.

"Disrespect will not be tolerated in this house, Annabel. Bubba Simpson's mother felt obliged to let me know that my own son managed to *in-gra-ti-ate* himself into the crime scene this morning."

Annabel felt gorge rising in her throat with Lilymae's prolonged drawl of the vowels in "ingratiate," but before she could respond, her mother turned away from Eliot and glared across the table at her daughter. "Go right ahead and zip your lips, Annabel. I have my own ways of finding out things to protect our good name," she added archly.

Eliot pushed back from the table and stalked out of the room without a word. Annabel stared silently at veal cutlets congealing in their own juice, until Lilymae stood, placed her knife, fork, and spoon in deliberate horizontal lines across her plate. She then swept majestically across the room, braced herself against the newel post, and stopped on the landing. Raising her voice to a near screech, she said: "Don't think I didn't see Willie Helms at the front door today, Annabel. I thought we'd seen the last of him. Decades ago."

Annabel hesitated before pushing against the screen door leading to the side porch where Eliot hunched into a swing that dared not move. The steady drone of cicadas made the sizzling July heat feel even more unbearable. Only bluntness could break the tension of this evening.

"Willie came here today. He thinks Orville wants to charge you with a crime." "A crime" sounded less threatening than "murder."

Eliot's utterance was a gutteral, hopeless statement. "He can. I fell in love with a sex slave."

"Never!" she responded more sharply than she intended, trying to find a formula for the words that would erase that stricken look from Eliot's face.

"Milo's slave. Imported from Croatia. Dream job in a free country. I was meant to save her. To save the child."

He shook his head in disbelief at his own frankness. "I was escaping with her, Annabel. Like teenagers on a sexual binge—planning a Grade B movie future. Too intimidated by Milo and his cartel goons, we were like fictional shipwrecked sailors," he paused. "So hopeful, but she was the one with the boat, saving a lonely old man stranded from life."

Eliot turned a plaintive face toward Annabel. "The pregnancy wasn't an anchor; it was a safe port. Then, it wasn't. One of the girls told Milo that Mirna was pregnant. He told Mirna that a baby the right color could bring $50,000—about what she would cost him for being out of the trade for six months. She had to run."

The naivete of Annabel's question startled her as soon as she asked it. "Why didn't she come here?"

"She couldn't. The first time I met her in that Ft. Worth bar, I had a running tab for drinks with my name and address. Mirna said Milo knew where to find me. One of the other girls, a friend of hers named Nadia, called to tell me that Mirna had done a runner and was safe until the baby came. Nadia told me to stay far away if I cared about Mirna."

Eliot dropped his head between his hands. "I did all the wrong things. I hired a stupid detective who confronted Milo in that bar and threatened to call

INS. Can you imagine a thug like Milo worried about deportation?"

Eliot began moving the swing slowly. "You should have seen Mirna. She looked ethereal, like one of those women in a Pre-Raphaelite painting, one of those sensual fallen angels." More like the old Eliot, he flashed her a quirky smile.

"I sound deranged, but the first time I saw her she was wearing this filmy, white dress that swirled about her under the overhead fan. She wore impossibly high heels. Her ankles were works of art. I was wearing that goofy tie you gave me—the one of Van Gogh's starry night. She looked at it and said: 'The fault, dear Brutus, is not in our stars, but in ourselves that we are underlings.'"

"Shakespeare in a sleazy bar and with a Slavic accent. It blew me away. Her pimp was glaring daggers at me, and I kept thinking: Why didn't I find this girl before? Before she became her own worst nightmare. Before she became mine."

The story that Eliot was telling took place somewhere in a bad world and had no good ending. In the distance, the cicadas drummed in sexual frenzy; all Annabel could think about was what she meant to say and what it would mean if she said it. And all she had said was: "Never." Half of that half-cocked raven's mantra from that opium-soaked brain of Poe.

Annabel felt that someone had just pushed her into a vat of slow-drying concrete; if she didn't struggle to free herself, she would turn into one of those tacky yard sculptures, grotesque and forever mute.

The sting of unsaid words gave an even more desperate air to the conversation she and her brother were *not* having.

"You really loved her?" She asked rather than stating the obvious. The words carried less weight as a question.

"I wanted her. I wanted the child. I wanted a different life." Eliot shoved his head against the chain holding up the swing, as though he longed for it to wrap itself around his neck.

Annabel felt like an ant separated from its beaten path, its antennae waving frantically and finding nothing around it familiar—just Eliot pushing the swing back and forth and staring into the distance.

After too many years of reticence, Annabel felt that she and her brother had just become intimate—but, at the same time, gauche. Eliot's grief drew them in, like a newly stitched wound that both repels and invites touch.

She had to fill in the silence with a small confession of her own. "I was in love once. Years and years ago. It was almost platonic—not quite, but almost." For more than two decades, she had managed to keep that single, fierce moment with Willie locked away. It seemed a foolish thing to say in the midst of her brother's hopelessness.

And there was that lost child. Such children were sometimes found. If not, the illusion of finding them always remained. These fatuous thoughts caused a terrible pain in her gut. Annabel felt like the Spartan boy silently holding a fox while it ate his entrails.

CHAPTER TWENTY-NINE

THE VIEWING

July 23, 1976

The phantasm in Eliot's head brought him to Vernica's door three days after the woman's body was found under the Hickory Creek Bridge. "You are the last person I know who talked with Mirna. You tried to help her. I just called the medical examiner in Ardmore. He says we can view her body, but he will keep it, pending the sheriff's release. I'd be indebted to you, Vernica, if you would go with me to see her."

The sterility of the room, the odor of disinfectants, the expressionless face of the ME, and Eliot's pallor should have prepared Vernica for the place of bodies in limbo. She always thought of the newly dead wandering around like Dante's lost souls on the shores of Acheron—until Goodin's Funeral Parlor could give them a nice tannish color for planting in Wolfe County soil.

When the ME whipped back the sheet, Vernica trembled. She rarely trembled, because life held no threat for someone as lonely as she had become in her old age. That young woman's face, as cold and pale as fine Italian marble, struck her with the unexpected force of bleakness.

Eliot had only told her that the girl was named Mirna and was from some place in Croatia. She watched him move his fingers along that frozen girl's face and whisper something that she could barely hear. Something about a detective from Ft. Worth and the word "baby."

On the drive back to Wolfe Flats, Eliot stared ahead as though transfixed by Highway 77 bleeding rivulets of tar into a jigsaw puzzle of what should be a state highway. His only comments were: "When they release her body, Mirna will be buried in our family plot. I'd like for you to be there with Annabel and me. Willie can come too."

He paused. "This Milo she mentioned to you, Vernica. He's the worst kind of criminal. He used to hang around a bar in Ft. Worth. The girls working there say no one has seen him for days. I intend to find him and kill him."

Vernica responded with a sharp intake of breath. The Poseys were not vengeful people. Eliot wouldn't shoot a mad dog. Annabel might, but only if she asked its pardon first. Vernica turned slightly to stare at Eliot's transfixed profile as he drove. Even as a boy, he carried an air of doom about him that was almost contagious, as though the silver spoon in his mouth tasted of tarnish.

"I don't understand why you say such a thing, Eliot. How do you know this Milo person is guilty?" Vernica's question was met with heavy silence. She had always considered her curiosity to be a form of charity, seeking to help or correct when nature went awry.

Her need to be helpful, to get to the bottom of things, sometimes got her in trouble in the classroom. Families in Wolfe Flats were like Mark Twain's moon—all of them with a dark side. But, Eliot had asked for her help by taking her to see the dead woman. Her question seemed in order. Yet, Eliot clutched the steering wheel and kept them inches away from the grassy verge.

His silence was rude; Eliot was often flippant but never rude. He had been an intensely private child, often staring silently at a blank canvas in her art class. When she asked what he was thinking, he would always say: "Great thoughts."

Absorbed in grief as he mindlessly steered the car along the ill-kept highway, Eliot could think only of Mirna with closed and sunken eyes in a cold room. Her eyes had been her most compelling feature, the way the light gathered in them as if he alone was meant to see the suffering there. Even then, they were eyes in which possibility no longer existed. He had longed to bring it back.

Vernica tried again. "Shouldn't you talk about this situation with Annabel or your mother?"

"Annabel in good time. Mother. Never!" The subject was closed.

He was right, of course. Without the restraining influence of Edward, the real Lilymae Posey surfaced before her husband's funeral flowers had wilted. Vernica had spotted her as a pretentious fool at the moment Edward Posey introduced his bride to her.

Disguising an almost clinical insecurity with her air of false sociability, Lilymae overwhelmed people with hospitality, and then punished them for perceived slights.

Vernica remembered those interminable musical soirées at the Posey house. When she thought no one was looking, Lilymae watched her guests with reptilian coldness, waiting for an opportunity to whisper: "Dear, you just spilled your punch on my Aubusson."

She lacked the vitality of someone purposefully cruel, someone able to draw in victims willingly. Harmless at her worst. A bore at her best. Yet, Vernica had endured Lilymae to stay close to the Posey family. Eliot and Annabel were like the children she never had. Affection meant staying the course with them, no matter how intolerable Lilymae had become without Edward's socially correct restraints.

Vernica scanned the horizon for the Wolfe Flats water tower, as Eliot sped along the lumpy highway, too fast for their safety. She felt an unbidden sense of anxiety but was determined to remain composed. Concealing emotions was a habit with Vernica. It put her in control, let her sort out the improbable, and bring reason back to the table.

She needed to talk with Annabel. Annabel might know something about Eliot's relationship to this dead woman. It would be best to get it into the open before the sheriff couldn't find a suspect and remembered his old grudges against Eliot.

CHAPTER THIRTY

DREAMS

The night that Annabel sat on the porch with Eliot, talking about a dead woman and her lost child, etched itself into her memory, the way a bad dream caught on the edge of waking nags at consciousness.

During the days that followed, Annabel watched her brother trying to think his way out of the problem of a lost child and a man he wanted to kill when the problem could not be solved by the way he was thinking.

Searching for physical traces of someone already dead was complicated by the fact that the woman didn't want to be found before she died. Until Mirna got off the bus in Wolfe Flats at noon on that Monday, no one had seen her for six months. Milo's girls refused to speak. The bar where they hung out had changed owners. Eliot's private investigators had followed every lead he could give them.

For the previous six months, Mirna had not been near the apartment that Eliot rented for her in Ft. Worth—the one Milo wasn't supposed to know about. Without a word, Mirna had left the room above the bar where four of Milo's girls shared twin beds and horror stories.

Milo raged. He blamed the bartender; he damaged his own goods with a nasty blow to the cheekbone of the girl called Nadia. One of the detectives had learned that much, but nothing else—before Mirna's transition from a frantic pregnant woman to a ghost—until she stepped off a Greyhound bus in Wolfe Flats.

Orville Bemis learned even less. The sheriff's one-man campaign against Eliot intensified with a series of orders that his deputy chose to ignore. Willie did visit Annabel that one time just to let her know that Orville was on the warpath. He also interviewed Eliot's CPA and two lawyers in Ardmore. Eliot's alibi for an all-day meeting the day of Mirna's visit to Wolfe Flats was ironclad. Annabel had taken her mother to a nerve specialist in Oklahoma City that day. The Poseys were in the clear.

Orville's next ploy was to attack the victim herself with not-so-subtle leaks to the press that mostly ignored him. He could not silence the Ardmore medical examiner, who released a statement regarding the fact that the strangled woman had recently given birth.

"Sold it. Or dropped it in the creek," Orville whispered to Peregrine Hamm at his drugstore, knowing those words would fester into a rumor within the hour.

The sheriff's official statement was more prudent, as befitted a man seeking a third term: "We can only trace the victim's actions from the time she got off the Greyhound and refused to make a complete statement in the Sheriff's Office. We cannot use limited resources in a fruitless search for what may not exist."

Eliot could and did. Two detectives from Oklahoma City canvassed the entire county, checked pickup registrations, and discovered that hardly anyone registered a pickup in Wolfe County. Ads for a missing baby proved useless. There was no description, no photograph, nothing but an account of an old-fashioned buggy that Vernica Roberts had seen in front of Selvige's.

As the weeks passed after Mirna's death, the initial sense of desperation that fired Eliot into a furious search had waned. Annabel could see him pushing the porch swing back and forth in the evenings, his mouth moving in a solitary dialogue with himself.

She dared not interrupt his speechless sadness. She read the weekly reports from the two detectives; they had nothing to report.

∽

Eliot did. On a hot morning near the end of August, Eliot raced down the spiral staircase two steps at a time and burst into the kitchen. "I had a dream, Annabel. It was so clear and so frightening. Like a message more than a dream. I was walking on a country road along a washed-out ditch. There was a blue baby blanket under some sticks and trash. I pulled it up and . . ." his voice broke.

Annabel looked away, her eyes filling with tears. She did not want to share this nightmare.

"There was nothing under the blanket but little lumps of decaying fat. Not even a skeleton. But it was a message. I know it was. I need to look for Mirna's baby, so whatever remains of it can be buried next to her."

Annabel nodded speechlessly. Putting a dead girl from Croatia next to their father in the family plot at Lakeview Cemetery had been distressing. Vernica and Willie were there, standing silently as the Episcopal priest from Gainesville said some things she couldn't remember.

She was startled to return to the gravesite two weeks later and find an austere black granite stone marked "Mirna" with July 19, 1976, under her name and the words of Emily Dickinson etched below:

> "I cannot live with You
> it would be Life

and Life is over there
Behind the Shelf."

Annabel had sunk down by the stark stone and the understated words and wept, as though she could not stop sobbing for a woman she had never met and a child who might not exist. Her emotions scattered like a broken string of beads, rolling out and away from her until she could gather then up with a new thread to hold them together. That thread was nowhere to be found.

Eliot's dream of finding the remains of Mirna's baby gave his days a purpose. Armed with a walking stick for poking through debris, Eliot took maps of the county and made careful grids across them, marking every road and every turnoff. He spent hours pacing county roads; every day he drove his car to the point where he had ended the previous day's search and started again.

After the third day of searching, Eliot took a big box of black plastic bags and exchanged his walking stick for a pole with a nail in the end of it. "The county roads are trashy. I can clean as I search." Every day, he hauled dozens of fat black bags to the dump. None of them held the bones of a missing baby.

By the time that heavy snow and sleet fell across the Oklahoma prairie, Eliot had completed his grid, leaving the landscape cleaner than it had been since the Great Depression, when no one had anything to throw away.

Six months later, Eliot's next dream startled his mother more than Annabel. "Golden chickens with long feathers like Phoenixes rising from the ashes were here in a large coop just behind the house. A baby was crying. I could hear Mirna's voice so clearly telling me that the chickens would save it."

"Chickens are stupid creatures, Eliot. They can't save themselves, much less a baby. What an imbecilic dream. I can't imagine why you'd tell us something so silly," Lilymae snorted in disgust.

Annabel could. Even though Eliot never mentioned Mirna or her lost child, she knew that he spent waking and sleeping hours trying to remember what he might have missed and what he must not forget. The cost of piping city water out to Mirna's grave was exhorbitant—so mounds of yellow roses could grow above her.

After telling Annabel and his mother about his dream of chickens, Eliot fell silent. For two days, he sat on the porch and stared into space. Then, he got on the phone with a fancy chicken breeder in Oklahoma City and ordered a dozen fertile eggs to be crated and sent by train to Wolfe Flats.

Tiny, yellowish Buff Orpingtons hatched beneath a Plymouth Rock hen. Coyotes nabbed several half-grown chicks one night, so Eliot hired a crew to build a large, fenced-in henhouse, and had them wire it for fans in the summer.

"Buff Orpingtons don't relish the heat," Eliot declared, as Annabel suggested putting water coolers in their own bedroom windows.

"They'd spoil the lines of the house," he retorted. So, the Poseys endured gyrating floor fans, just like Eliot's great golden prize rooster.

As a gentleman farmer with herds of registered cattle, fields of mixed breed steers fattening for the market, and bottomlands teeming with wild turkey, quail, and imported pheasants, Eliot occupied himself with chickens—aristocratic, golden Buff Orpingtons.

Annabel could see him wearing an ascot, like a deranged British lord, tossing cracked corn to his chickens, his yellow silk socks hanging like pudding around his thin ankles.

At least he was home. Annabel remembered those weekly absences when Eliot had been driving to Ft. Worth. She recalled the irritation she had felt then, knowing that he was participating in a secretive life, lived in brief intervals outside the Queen Anne cage of their house. It wasn't jealousy she felt, only a kind of force field of emotion from which she was excluded.

If that life could only come back to her brother, that air of anticipation he had carried about with him for such a brief time, Annabel felt she could be happy. Instead, she watched him moving from one manic phase to another. First, the endless walking of country roads, raking through debris, bagging everything he could find, except a blue baby blanket.

Now the chickens. They ate the eggs, but not the chickens. The chickens were personal. They had names: Biblical names like Sarah, Bathsheba, Esther, and Rebeccah. The solitary rooster was called Hosanna for his clarion call. "Like the chorus from Beethovan's Mass. Disruptive." The slight quirk at the corner of Eliot's mouth as he stared at their mother reminded Annabel that her brother once had a sense of humor.

Presently, she rarely saw any evidence of it, as he spent more and more time with bottles of Jack Daniels—tucked into hay stacks in the barn, under the seat of his car, and in large, water-sized glasses after dinner at night.

Annabel watched his self-contempt grow, as the weeks stretched into months with no information about Mirna's missing baby and no trace of a man called Milo. Eliot seemed to be able to endure himself without loathing as long as a bottle was near at hand. It was nothing like the alcoholic binges of his youth, when Dutch courage was needed to scale the town water tower or plunge into the Red River in flood stage.

Eliot's need for alcohol now helped him reach a state of disembodiment before he could fall into the blessed coma of drunkenness. There were no refining fires in his suffering, just residual ash. Annabel felt choked by it.

A year later, after Lilymae's stroke, Eliot stopped drinking so much. He still had his nightly glass of whiskey, dark as over-brewed tea. He no longer drank to excess.

CHAPTER THIRTY-ONE

THE STROKE

June 3, 1977

The grayish images of that night were riveted in Annabel's memory, the way that a fixative spray sets a charcoal drawing against smudging.

Vernica had asked Annabel to her house for dinner and a game of Scrabble. Lilymae hadn't felt well all day and peevishly complained: "Your friend imposes on us, Annabel. She spurns my little gatherings, says that she doesn't have time to be *in–volv–ed*." The word came out in three syllables. Annabel knew her mother could be savage when she thought someone failed to recognize her as the doyenne of Wolfe Flats by refusing an invitation.

"The only possible reason for you to spend time with Vernica must be your admiration for her new hairdo. It looks like overcooked meringue. You would do her a kindness to advise her to sue the beauty shop."

Annabel couldn't think of a retort. The move from a Macon, Georgia, parsonage that her father did not own to her husband's Queen Anne house brought the taste of privilege for which Lilymae imagined she was born—and fed her callous disregard of others.

"I'll be here with Mother, Annabel. You go ahead and enjoy your evening." Eliot's words were so slurred that she could hardly sort them out, but Annabel had gratefully escaped.

When she returned just after ten o'clock, Annabel was startled to see the lights blazing over dirty dishes on the dinner table. Her mother did not permit disorder in the household. Plates were always cleared and left to soak for the cook. Lights were dimmed after dinner.

The raspy snoring of Eliot masked the faint whimpers of her mother sprawled alongside her chair. One pale, spindly leg extended from beneath the chair, as though the fake Louis XVI had sprouted another limb.

The numbness on one side of her body, the faint trail of drool along her chin, and her inability to speak clearly did not hide the fury in her mother's eyes.

Annabel stared down at her, unable to move or cry out, as she watched her mother flap one arm and one foot helplessly among the folds of her blue satin robe. The image that came to Annabel was of an anemone, anchored to coral, with little clown fish moving into its waving fronds, unable to move far from its tentacles.

Eliot, escaping with a bottle, and Annabel, vanishing into a Scrabble game, were the clown fish. Their mother, gasping on the floor, was a predatory polyp.

After forty years of taking to her bed with imaginary but rare medical conditions, Lilymae followed a mundane path in recovering from what she described as a "debilitating stroke." The immediate effects of her stroke subsided quickly. Lilymae's anger at Annabel did not. A less than functional left hand and a slight limp were the major aftermaths of the stroke.

One drooping eyelid convinced Lilymae that her face was akilter, destroying her social life—without too much impact on Wolfe Flats. For years, a select group of women from town had endured her weekly teas and her spirited *Für Elise*. Gossip tempered the pain of the music.

The music stopped, but the gossip would always continue. Wolfe Flats nourished its affliction for tittle-tattle that passed through knotholes in fences and over cornrows in backyard gardens faster than a riled hornet.

The new granite tombstone in the Posey family plot bearing the name "Mirna" fed a spate of interesting conjecture about Eliot Posey; rumors traveled in waves of speculation about the murder of a foreign woman. The notion that a baby had been snatched off Main Street went the way of idle speculation.

In time, a grain elevator explosion and the birth of a two-headed calf claimed headlines of the weekly paper, leaving Lilymae moored to her invalid state and her children to their reclusive lives.

Weeks after her stroke sent her into retreat, Lilymae thumped loudly down the great twisted ramp of stairs, like an out-of-step member of a marching band, and proclaimed: "I will not be seen in public. It's tiresome to have one's ill health be fodder for discussion. Family pride will not allow my daughter's failings to be a source of common gossip."

Annabel never questioned why her mother held her responsible for an erratic blood clot. The fact that Eliot was at home and in a drunken stupor during his mother's crisis was never mentioned.

Like a cabal of tattlers without their mean-spirited leader, the social group that Lilymae had cultivated for four decades in the name of music and a few rubbers of bridge dissipated quickly, with no more ado than a round of soggy casseroles delivered to the Posey house in the hope of seeing the altered face of the late hostess.

After Lilymae's dismissal of a series of trucu-
lent nurse aides, life at the Posey house returned to
old patterns. Eliot relied on Hiram and his tenants
to manage the crops and livestock, while he spent
a minimum amount of time with accountants. He
spent a maximum amount of time wandering aimlessly along Hickory Creek.

With the exception of the obligatory visits by Hiram
and Maudie, the only regular caller to the Posey
Queen Anne house was Vernica. Vernica's grandfather had been a Royal Arch Mason, buried in Lakeview Cemetery behind a column almost as imposing as the Leaning Tower of Pisa. Lilymae armed
herself with the forebearance and cold civility due a
member of Wolfe Flats' old guard.

The games of Scrabble that Vernica *forced* on
Annabel were annoying. Lilymae begrudged the
three-way conversations among Eliot, Annabel, and
Vernica about "interiors" and "Bonnard and Vuillard."
They seemed to be speaking in tongues, like some of
her daddy's brush arbor converts.

From a straight-backed chair shoved against
the wall, Lilymae watched them like a marginalized
potentate, as Eliot, once again, brought up the tedious
subject of getting a Caulder mobile to replace the
Venetian glass chandelier in the parlor. Rinky-dinky
pieces of colored metal wired together by a man who
had hoodwinked the art world. Not in her parlor.

Not while she had a breath in her body to protect her Murano glass.

"Mother, why don't you join us? Have one of these nice muffins that Maudie brought over," Annabel patted the stiff brocaded settee next to Vernica. With her left eye partially obscured by a drooping lid, her mother's right eye had taken on a bright, spherical appearance—like that of a fly with a 360 range of vision. Not missing a thing.

"I've had a sufficiency. My invalided leg prefers a straight chair. Chat away. I'll be no bother. As always." Lilymae caught just the twitch of Vernica's upper lip before it composed itself into a neutral expression. She watched Annabel's poker face, giving away nothing. Only Eliot rolled his eyes upward, as though imploring heaven. Obvious slights from Eliot she could forgive. Her frozen-faced daughter needed dressing down.

Without the curb of Vernica or Eliot around, the strength of Lilymae's viperish tongue always returned two-fold to remind Annabel of her failings. "I had to outwit the miserable circumstances of my youth." Lilymae cocked her good eye toward the east and squinted, as though watching the panorama of her youth in the tents and brush arbors of Georgia evangelical furor unfold like forgettable credits on a movie screen.

"You wouldn't understand my childhood, Annabel. You grew up without circumstances."

The best defense against her mother's sibylline pronouncements was silence. Annabel had learned to master it. As she put away the Scrabble board, she shot her mother a hostile glance and wondered how this aging woman with a drooping eye and useless arm managed to keep her adult children in orbit around her for so many years.

Their acquiescence was pathological. Of that Annabel was sure. Her own memories were stratified by her father's early death. He had understood the silence of an inner life that is too rare for sharing. That life for her might have been comfort enough until she experienced Eliot's despair over Mirna. Now, events outside her control commandeered her thoughts and emotions.

The only positive outcome of her mother's stroke was Eliot's resumption of his old life—working with Hiram to keep the Posey estate intact for no one to inherit and a passion only for his Buff Orpingtons.

CHAPTER THIRTY-TWO

LIMERICKS

Wednesday, July 18, 1981

Annabel watched her mother scrutinizing Eliot and Ave across the table. She would be plotting her usual morning smattering of small talk, full of sly innuendoes, avoiding talking about anything that really mattered, such as a stray child under their roof.

It wasn't just her mother, thought Annabel. Small talk is the Wolfe Flats vernacular, a way of avoiding the bad taste that can underlie direct statements.

Her mother made one that startled Ave: "Why were you hiding with the chickens?"

"Because they has wings." Shocked by her own outburst, the child moved back into her role as a mime by zipping her thumb and forefinger across her mouth, as she stared Lilymae into an uncomfortable silence.

Eliot flipped the pages of Edward Lear's book and announced:

> "There was a Young Lady of Hull,
> Who was chased by a virulent bull;
> But she seized on a spade,
> And called out, 'Who's afraid?
> Which distracted that virulent bull."

Not afraid, but desperately unsettled, Annabel pushed back her chair, touched the top of Ave's head bent over a book that was not nonsensical at all, and walked out to the front porch.

The copper rain gutters on the turrets at each end of the tall roof flashed a greenish hue in the morning sun. Annabel's father said he built a tower for each of his children so they would have a "magical" place.

Remembering her own childhood struck Annabel with an odd sense of melancholy, like leafing through old photograph albums and finding a pop-up valentine tender with sentiment but foxed brown about the edges.

She felt a sharp pain between her ribs, as though her heart were closing in on itself to counter memories she knew that small child sitting at the kitchen table had never experienced.

During those summers of her childhood, her father—as firm as Agamemnon—set his children on a course of freedom to roam his thousand acres, so that they would grow up loving this land looped by the Red River.

Annabel frowned at the comparison of her father to a tragic Mycenae king. She should have known back then that the Gods would resent such happiness and demand a sacrifice—not his stalwart, thick-legged, misnamed daughter—her father's own faulty aorta.

The Greek tragedy ended there on the front porch and the comedy began. Annabel smiled ruefully. Her mother had not become so much like herself while her father was alive to temper her demands. "No, Lilymae, our children's summer will not be music lessons and church camps. I know the ladies in your club don't agree. Our children's lives will be structured soon enough. Too soon." Annabel remembered the sense of doom she felt with those words.

Those were halcyon days, while their father lived and Eliot preferred their make-believe world, before the town boys and, later, the girls intruded.

The fatally flawed Greeks were Eliot's favorites. Climbing to the top of the roof, he would shout: "Now I shall go to overtake that killer, Hector; then I will accept my own death, at whatever time Zeus wishes to bring it about." Annabel always played Hector, weighed down by her father's old raccoon coat, shouting: "My doom has come upon me," as her brother whacked her with a wooden sword.

When Eliot was in a conciliatory mood, he consented to be Priam, watching the Greeks coming in waves through the Big Bluestem, while Annabel shrieked prophecies from the top of the silo. Even now, Annabel remembered how she loved being Cassandra—so mad, so misunderstood, so right.

In the morning breeze, standing at the edge of the porch and looking out across the prairie, Annabel recalled how—even as a young girl with her hair streaming in the summer winds—she felt her life playing out.

Now, she heard sounds coming from the kitchen, where Ave had not stopped listening or eating. Annabel couldn't remember being that young; what she did remember was a persistent, childhood fear that their lives would end in a terrible muddle.

Eliot was too much like the Greeks, plunging along on his own path, caught up with a doomed woman, and no clear understanding of what threads were being chopped off in the heavens above. Annabel sighed and moved resolutely back towards the kitchen.

Her mother had scooted into the chair on the left-hand side of Eliot and was listening with a childlike intensity as he read. From this distance, her slightly misshapened face looked almost youthful. Annabel remembered how forbearing her father had been in dealing with his wife's mercurial temper. "She has such a sweet, heart-shaped face."

Annabel felt a tinge of guilt. At the time, she thought her mother's face resembled the triangular head of a Praying Mantis, the sort that eats the head off her mate as he mounts her.

Annabel walked softly down the hall and looked through the kitchen door. Eliot turned the pages as he pretended to read to Ave. The stories were not coming from Edward Lear. They were stories about growing up with barns full of baby animals and trees that invited children to climb heavenward.

At that moment, Annabel could see Eliot at ten or eleven, threshing the Big Bluestem about with a branch of Bois D'Arc for a sword, assured that, like Achilles, only his heel was vulnerable. While their father cheered him on like a Greek chorus, their mother watched behind the curtain of an upstairs window, planning small reprisals.

Annabel turned away from the door so that Ave could not see the sudden pain reflected on her face. Like Agamemnon, falling under the knife of his wife, her father had crumpled with a trampled heart. It had her mother's footprints all over it.

CHAPTER THIRTY-THREE

ANOTHER VISIT

Friday, July 20, 1981

The rattle of Admah Reave's truck alerted Annabel to danger before Eliot's Buff Orpington rooster squawked from the turret overlooking his coop of hens. She hustled Ave into the kitchen cupboard and watched her curl herself into invisibility. There was no need to warn her into silence. Fear made its home in that child's eyes.

Annabel opened the front door but kept the screen closed between her and the powerfully built man standing on her porch. She recognized Admah Reave and that strange, brutish boy of his who slumped along the edge of the porch, his huge hands swinging almost to his knees.

Everyone in Wolfe Flats knew about the Reave clan; their social seclusion, religious extremism, and suspected polygamy made them as alien as a band of bonobos.

Annabel's own moral pluralism might have allowed her to open the door to a neighbor—even one she had never formally met—but she was unnerved by the feral expression on that odd boy's face as he sniffed around the periphery of the porch.

"What can I do for you, Mr. Reave?" Annabel kept one eye on the boy who flashed a sinister grin at her.

"Me and my boy Hoser are looking for my girl that's run off. She's his half-sister. Our dogs followed her scent to those trees over there," he gestured toward the barrier of poplar trees that screened the house from the road. "We think she's hiding in one of your barns or sheds."

"She ain't, Pa. She's inside. She never could hide from me," Hoser blurted out. With one hand on the ornate railing, he swung up to the porch with the ease of an ape, tugged at the crotch of his jeans, and moved toward the door.

Annabel watched Hoser's tongue licking the sharp crags of his front teeth like a wild beast that has just finished a bloody meal and is anticipating the next one. She instinctively moved back, fighting the urge to slam the door and hide with Ave, and thought: *this creature is not the blood kin of that desperate child hiding in the cupboard. Finding her is a sport for him.*

Sensing her alarm, Admah Reave thrust out his leg, blocked Hoser from moving closer, and shoved him back onto the porch rail.

Frowning at his glowering son, Admah said apologetically. "My boy's been upset since Betty Heather run off. The girl belongs to us. I've been sheltering her for five years. We don't want trouble, Miz Posey. We just want what is ourn. That's justice."

Annabel and Admah eyed each other with mutual incomprehension. To Annabel, justice should balance her scales on the side of a fragile child cowering inside the house. She knew that Admah's moral compass swung wide of that mark. Justice for him meant getting back his property. His use of the word "sheltering" brought up bile in her throat, as an image of Ave's thin, bruised body flashed before her.

Her flash of outrage startled her. Annabel's first thought was to look straight into the eyes of Admah Reave with a weapon in her hand; her second thought was to wonder how she could reach into that pool of darkness that those eyes hid and close them forever. That terrified child in the closet deserved more than the pretense that was taking place on both sides of a screen door. Ave's entire life had been a deception because of this man, standing before her, hat in hand.

From the front parlor, Schumann's "Ave Maria" played on the old Victrola. Lilymae refused to use the tape player. She said tapes "lacked solidity." With a "touch" of deafness that Lilymae denied, she liked turning up the amplifier so she could feel the vibrations of the music.

When Annabel thought of Ave as a name for that damaged child hiding in the henhouse, she had made no connection to the Virgin Mary. It appeared that Lilymae had.

"Foul demons of the earth and air from their wanted haunt exiled." The lyrics of the song struck Annabel with an unexpected force. This house seemed to be a fortress, but she knew that the enemy was without, peering through the screen door.

Now was not the time to show any emotion, especially fear. That impassive face of Admah Reeve hid a keen and resolute intelligence that could spot a lie in a heartbeat. Enigmatic as the Sphinx, Annabel measured her response carefully. "No child of yours is in this house." Technically speaking, she had not lied. A man who spawned a creature like Hoser never fathered that bruised child hiding inside.

Unable to control her anxiety for a moment longer, Annabel closed the heavy front door with a thunderous finality.

As Admah stomped across the yard toward the pickup, he glared at Hoser. "You shoulda stayed in the truck like I told you. Town people are always suspicious of us. You scared that Posey woman. Poseys are not to be trifled with. She won't let us look in those barns now."

"I could find Betty Heather in a heartbeat. She's in that house. I know it for a certainty. I done sniffed her out."

Watching his son inhaling like a bluetick hound on the scent, an uncomfortable feeling settled upon Admah; then, Hoser made it worse.

"If we come back after dark, I'll get in that side window with the loose screen before them folks know it. Be out of there with her before the shake of a stick."

"And get yourself arrested for breaking into a rich man's house. They'd send you to Big Mac before you could whistle Dixie. Sometimes you act dumb as a post, Hoser. Nope. We're going to see Sheriff Beamis. Do this thing right. He'll get a search warrant. He owes us for all those bargains on cars."

Admah pursed his lips and looked doubtfully back at the huge Queen Anne house. "Can't imagine why folks that rich would want someone else's troublesome child."

Hoser didn't answer his pa. He had seen them pale blue eyes like Betty Heather's one time—just before death closed them five years ago down by the Hickory Creek bridge. He still remembered the reassuring thump of roadkill under the wheels of that Pontiac Firebird. The sheriff would never know he owed him for taking care of a woman killer, one with greasy hair, black as a hunk of coal.

On the ride into Wolfe Flats, Admah began to have doubts about going to the sheriff. For good reasons, the Reaves never took their problems to the law. Thinking back to his Lazarus baby niggled under his skin worse than scabies. From the moment his father, Abner, had lifted a pink and golden child from that coffin on the altar and troubled heaven with his shouts, Admah knew that trouble would visit his house; some days, he no longer had the will to resist it.

The miracle of a healthy baby replacing that stone cold, lumpy-headed sickly thing that Wilmy birthed was beyond belief. Wilmy accepted the miracle without question. If the dead could be raised, their hair and eyes could change color.

After the agonizing birthing process and the first death of her baby, dullness had settled on Wilmy, as though her spirit was decomposing, even as she went through the motions of mothering the risen baby.

Dodging potholes on the long stretch of road from the Posey house, Admah drove carefully along the rutted gravel tracks before turning onto Highway 77, still thinking about Wilmy. In bed, his second wife was compliant as a lump of dough when the yeast is dead.

His first wife Essie cared about him; even after seven stillborn babies, she held him close at night. Wilmy only tolerated him, with a kind of sullen acquiescence that sometimes took the spirit right out of him.

After the baby came, a flash of Wilmy's old spirit occasionally flared against Hoser, who had once been her only ally. "Don't touch that soft spot on her head!"

Admah had watched Hoser's thumb caress the fontanelle on the baby's head, thinking that one slip and her brain would be mush. Things were calmer when he didn't confront his son.

Admah knew that the possessive gleam in Hoser's eyes when he dangled the baby too high unsettled his wife. Docile as a milk cow that knows its own stall, Wilmy didn't complain about the crowded space in their lean-to; she just closed in on herself, watched Hoser like a hawk, and didn't want Betty Heather to be out of her sight.

Admah kept long hours in the fields and had little time for that bright flash of insolence that he should think of as his daughter. He was fond of Betty Heather. How could he not be? She walked at nine months and talked in complete sentences before she was two. At three, she could make out the words in the storybook before Wilmy sounded them out for her. By the time she was four, Betty Heather began to give a wide berth to Hoser. That's when Admah started to ponder over a change that Hoser wouldn't like.

By the time that boys in the Reave clan reached their early teens, they moved into the Sleep Shed, a long room lined with beds under the roof of a barn where hay was no longer stored; the only amenity was a Spark Pot Belly stove and a zinc washtub with bars of lye soap and washrags.

Hoser should have moved in with the other boys when the baby came, but he found excuses about helping Wilmy, because she was poorly after her birthing ordeal.

The subject of moving to the Sleep Shed came up one evening as Admah watched Hoser at the dinner table. Like a sword swallower pushing food down his throat fast enough to squelch the flames, Hoser reached for a third hunk of cornbread and swatted a small hand extended for the same piece. "Mine, Betty Heather. I'll play you a game tonight for it."

Admah watched the child slump down with the kind of fear that a mistreated dog shows. He should have taught Hoser table manners years ago. Something else gnawed at Admah, like a bad tooth, annoying, but only symptomatic of something worse to come.

"You shouldn't slap that child's hand when she reaches for food, Hoser. She's too skinny. She needs to eat more—not be punished." Admah looked across the table into a tiny child's wide blue eyes that revealed absolutely nothing.

"That little smack didn't hurt. I only punish her for her own good. So she won't be gettin' into the wrong things," Hoser added piously. He had taken Betty Heather that very morning to show her how one chicken had picked out the eye of another. It had been a valuable lesson.

"Don't never let on yore hurt. That's when they git you." He had his own methods for teaching this ungrateful child, who had begun to shrink from his hands like those little ferns in the woods that folded in when stroked.

Admah had looked sternly at his son stuffing in another hunk of cornbread. "I think it's time you moved into the shed with the boys your age. We're tripping over each other here. Betty Heather is too old to be sleeping in our room. She can sleep in your space in the kitchen."

Hoser had looked up at his father under hooded eyes. "I didn't do nothin'."

Admah knew that meant Hoser had perpetrated considerable mayhem. "I didn't say you did. It ain't a punishment, Hoser. You're a grown boy. Folks talk when we don't follow our own rules. You need to be with the other boys."

Hoser pushed back from the table, grabbed his quilt and pillow, and shot a hateful look back at Betty Heather as he pushed open the door. She was way overdue a punishment. She was getting too sassy and too grabby for her own good—a prissy little thing that took up all of Wilmy's time. Wilmy had taught her to read books he couldn't read until he was twice her age.

When his pa wasn't around, he had the right to punish her. Hoser's mouth twisted into that half smile that made people keep their distance. Years ago, he had done that miracle, with all the folks praising his grandpa like he was some kind of saint.

He had moved like a shadow that night, switching the living for the dead, and hiding the dead in a shallow grave. Now that Wilmy was so puny in her mind, Betty Heather was his responsibility.

This moving to the shed business didn't just come out of thin air. Hoser frowned. He didn't like boys his own age. He liked living with Wilmy under the same roof; hearing the thump of his pa in bed with her at night excited him.

Sleeping alongside a dozen snorting boys kept him in a piss-poor mood.

Hoser glared defiantly at his pa easing the truck down the road from the Posey house and turning cautiously onto Highway 77, slow as an old man. If Pa hadn't been with him this morning, he could have pushed that woman aside and found Betty Heather. He needed to be the first to find her and give her a warning.

Hoser mulled over the past two days. Two nights before, Pa had come in late from hauling a load of steers to the auction barn in Wolfe Flats and found Betty Heather curled up next to Wilmy.

She had run off that morning, but Hoser found her down by the creek and shook her until her teeth rattled for upsetting Wilmy. Wilmy didn't seem grateful when he brought her home; she started crying in that strange, half-hearted way she had of weeping. Betty Heather didn't say a word.

When his pa had come back that night, he looked tired, shucked off his boots, and moved aside the curtain where Wilmy and Betty Heather eyed him like an intruder. Outside, Hoser stayed glued to the window, uneasy about the welts on the child that should have gone away by now.

He watched his pa pick up the girl and take her into the kitchen. "Why do you make your mama cry by running away? She's not well." When he set her on the table, the coal oil lamp threw odd shadows across her arms, making the bruises appear worse than they were. "Who done this to you?"

Betty Heather wrapped her thin arms across the reddened stripes and refused to answer. Hoser watched his pa rummaging through a drawer in the cabinet; he picked up a small lock, grabbed Betty Heather's pallet, wrapped an arm around her, and headed toward the door.

"I'm putting you in a safe place in the old shed tonight so you can't run off. I'll lock the door so no one can get in, but your mama needs some rest. I'll bring you some supper after I've done the chores. Then we'll get to the bottom of this." Betty Heather dangled under his arm like a rag doll as he rounded the corner of the house.

The moment his pa left to do chores, Hoser slipped into the house and filched the key. "Getting to the bottom of this" might put him into hot water with Pa. Now that he no longer lived in the house with Betty Heather, she was out of control. Showing off when she wasn't running off. He would just have a little talk with her in the shed about keeping her mouth shut before Pa came back with her supper.

∽

As his pa wheeled onto the main street and parked alongside the courthouse door that led down a hall to the Sheriff's Office, Hoser experienced a tinge of regret thinking about what he might have done to Betty Heather. Not that she didn't deserve it for hiding again and frustrating him when he was frantic to be out of the shed before Pa came with her supper.

When he had aimed the flashlight at her pallet, she wasn't on it; he poked around every corner of the shed; by the time he found her perched on a low rafter, he was out of control. That child made him uneasy, always watching with those eyes the color of the clearest blue sky, the kind of sky under which nothing could be hidden.

He might have rubbed against her too hard. But truth be told, he assured himself, they's worse things in store for her when she gets more size on her. It was a kindness to prepare her for what lay ahead of her. He had seen the shocked eyes of heifers when the bull mounted them. It was dark; Betty Heather couldn't see nothin'. She likely wouldn't remember.

A vast sense of relief settled on Hoser as his pa stepped out of the pickup and motioned him to wait. His pa's frustration at finding a good sheet torn up and a hole punched through the rotten roof of the shed had turned his anger toward Betty Heather. That's where Hoser wanted it to roost.

CHAPTER THIRTY-FOUR

VISITING THE SHERIFF

A dmah Reave's visit to the Sheriff's Office broke precedent. The Reave clan avoided any official contact with the law, because they tampered with it so often. Deputy Helms lifted one eyebrow as Admah edged up to his desk, hat in hand, his fingers like a fleet of hungry moths working the felt trilby.

"You handle Admah Reave," Sheriff Bemis had muttered as he slunk out the back door of the office. That meant Orville didn't want any grievance of the Reave family to end up at his official door. Those stripped-down, repainted cars and trucks didn't just move across the state line without Orville getting an occasional trade-in.

The deputy stared into a pair of muddy brown eyes under a supraorbital ridge that seemed designed to hide secrets; he gestured toward the chair across from his desk. Admah stepped back.

"I won't take a seat, Deputy Helms. I'm here on personal business. My girl run off, and I think the Poseys got her. The dogs traced her to the edge of the tree line on their road. A Posey woman—I think she's the daughter—slammed the door in my face this morning." Admah flushed with the remembrance of the woman's piercing look, as though she knew more than he would ever want her to know.

"I'll need to take down some information, Mr. Reave." Willie Helms pulled out a pad and stopped. "Why in the world would you accuse the Poseys of such a thing?" He asked incredulously.

"The scent was strong. Our dogs tracked her. My son Hoser and I followed her trail from out in the West End clear up past the line of trees by the Posey house. When I knocked politely on the door to inquire if they might have seen her, Miz Posey did not act neighborly to me and my boy."

The deputy glanced out the half-basement window. He could see Hoser Reave squatting by the side of a pickup. Hoser had a reputation of sorts in Wolfe Flats, the reputation of an aggressive primate that no one wants to test. Willie could not imagine a daughter with the same brutish appearance.

"Description? Age? Time of day she went missing?" The deputy's pen was poised for a brief documentation of a teenage runaway, hostile, angry, and eager to cause chaos at home.

"Whitish hair. Eyes so pale blue that the light goes right through them. Skinny. I'd say thirty or forty pounds wet. Five years old. She escaped some-time Tuesday night."

"Escaped?" Deputy Helms had not written a word. He had never seen a blond, blue-eyed Reave. Once basically reclusive, the Reave clan now came into Wolfe Flats for things they couldn't grow or steal; the stocky Reave women sold baked goods and vege-tables at the Farmers' Market in the summer and fall.

"Not like tied up, Deputy. I made her a nice lit-tle bed in a shed because Wilmy, her ma, is poorly. The shed was locked so she'd be safe." Admah Reave looked like a man on the first step of the gallows.

"Safe? From what?"

Watching nervous fingers working his hat and his feet rooted to the floor, the deputy could spot the lie before it came out of Admah's mouth.

"Betty Heather run off Tuesday morning when I was in the fields. Hoser, her brother . . ." he paused. "Half brother. He disciplined her. We're not a-spare-the-rod kind of folks, Deputy. But Hoser sometimes don't know his own strength. I fixed her a little room in the shed where she wouldn't be both-ered and could give some thought to the grief she was causing her ma."

Admah moved forward until his muscular thighs bumped the edge of the desk. "When I took her supper out to her, I saw that she had cut up a good sheet, climbed through the roof, and swung down to the ground."

"Hoser and me got the dogs out, after all of us searched the places where she might hide. Our folks take strong against children not minding. I've been doing for that girl for five years. I want her back."

Years of being the Deputy Sheriff, weighing what he believed to be the truth against what Sheriff Bemis declared to be true, had fine-tuned Willie Helms' internal lie detector.

"What I don't understand, Mr. Reave, is why you locked a young child in a shed by herself at night. Just how did your son *discipline* her?" The question hit Admah like the sting of a hornet.

"Better still. Call your boy in here. I want to hear his answer."

Admah Reave stood on one side of a deep, emotional ravine; one wrong word and he'd plunge into the void. Hoser could not be questioned. Attention made him self-important. He would say the wrong thing. It was time to appeal to the deputy's sense of fairness.

"I don't aim to be taking up your valuable time with my trouble, Deputy Helms. Wilmy, my wife, she's not been right." He touched his temple. "She's puzzled. Been that way when we thought she lost the baby . . . going on five years now. The Lord restored her child, but she can't seem to accommodate to . . ." he paused. "She's over-protective and the child acts out, runs off, tries everyone's patience. Upsets her ma no end."

As he half-listened to Admah Reave rattling on, Willie had focused on only one thing Admah had let slip, almost as an afterthought: "going on five years now." That date would always stick in his head. It was the last time that he had knocked on Annabel Posey's door, sent by the sheriff to ask about her brother's relationship to that foreign woman who was murdered down by Hickory Creek.

"I don't want to sign no paperwork, Deputy," Admah's voice trembled with frustration. "I want the law to do what's fair. Just go check the Posey property to be sure my girl ain't hiding there. Get a search warrant or something."

"We most certainly can do that, Admah. Sorry I couldn't deal with you myself. I was called out on other business." A line of gravy the shape of the Erie Canal trailed down the front of Sheriff Bemis' shirt, a testament to "other business."

"My deputy knows the Poseys well, don't you Willie? I'll bet we can make them listen to reason. We surely won't need a search warrant. You handle it, Deputy."

Orville Bemis ignored the baleful glance that his deputy sent him. He threw an arm across Admah's shoulder and steered him to the door. "That turbo engine in the Bonneville you found me is causing me a world of trouble when . . ."

Willie Helms shuffled the paper on his desk. He could envision a "world of trouble" when he confronted Annabel with Admah Reave's request for a search of her property. It was a ridiculous request. The Poseys wouldn't conceal someone's child.

His sharp intake of breath startled him. Five years ago, Eliot Posey spent a tortured six months of his life combing the ditches along county roads, looking for that dead woman's baby. After bouts of heavy drinking, Eliot slipped back into his old life. But, he was never quite the same.

A slight smile eased Willie's frown. Annabel was the same. He sometimes caught a glimpse of her around town, talking to other people, her lips just on the edge of being faintly disappointed, as though a single word from the right person could flip them into a smile. Her skin retained a peach-like texture, as though middle age had decided to pass her by—although the faint creases flaying out from her Delph-blue eyes told another story.

Willie pushed back his chair and stared into space. As a young girl, Annabel had the most bewitching smile. Time had not changed that—or the vision that flickered in his head, like one of those faulty reel-to-reel films, image imposed upon image.

Annabel, tarted up with layers of tulle, moving her sturdy legs across that makeshift dance floor the night of their high school graduation. Annabel, her net skirts prickly as thistles, moving against him in the bed of his pickup, as though the stars they lay beneath predestined their coupling—a destiny cut short by his parents' skid across an icy highway.

On the way to the Posey house that afternoon, memories as soft and persistent as a first snowfall tumbled through Willie's mind. He had been the first to arrive and the last to leave the graduation party at the Posey's all those years ago.

The memories remained fresh: an altercation on the dance floor with Orville; one side of the rented tent dangling askew like Annabel's net petticoats; lying on a scratchy wool army blanket on the rippling metal of a pickup bed under a starry canopy; and, Annabel naming the constellations as though she were chanting a canticle as a blessing.

He had moved into her with such stealth and speed that he could only breathe Emily Dickinson's words into her ear: "Wild Nights—Wild Nights! Were I with thee Wild Nights would be our luxury."

His next memory was of his hands doing something strange to the layers of net petticoats that made Annabel look like an over-sized, upside-down dandelion. Ironing. He had been ironing, trying to smooth the recalcitrant net back into order under her flounced skirt.

"We can get married, Annabel. Soon as I get my degree. Sooner if we have to."

"Annabel!" Her mother's voice had come wailing into the night like a banshee's from her post on the front porch. "I can see Willie Helms's pickup is still here. Your party is over. He needs to go home."

With that recollection, a sheepish smile appeared on Willie's face, as he circled the rose bed at the side of the house that hadn't changed much in all these years. He had gone home to avoid facing Annabel's mother, his mouth full of promises.

A promise he had never expected to make to his dead parents intruded, as he stood dry-eyed by two gleaming caskets and comforted three sobbing younger brothers.

That winter afternoon, Annabel had watched them at the gravesite without saying a word. A quartet of grief is symmetrical. The axis must be canted to accommodate a fifth person. Willie could see the quiet understanding in Annabel's eyes, the knowledge that she would go away to college and to another life, and he would stay in Wolfe County.

He stayed, cared for his brothers, and used the small income from the farm to make better lives for them; he did not expect or receive gratitude.

Annabel didn't go far—just an hour over to Durant, embarrassing her mother, who would have been happier if her daughter had exiled herself in Elba. Except for the token holiday visits, four years passed before Annabel came home to stay.

Eliot had come back from Harvard then. As they had done in their childhood, they isolated themselves once again.

Willie crunched the brake and stared at the Queen Anne behind a curved, gravel drive; the pretentious house on this Oklahoma prairie had taken on a quaint air as it aged—much like its inhabitants, except for Mrs. Posey. Nothing was whimsical about that bizarre woman.

Willie thought back to that last day in the fourth grade when the principal had come for Annabel to go home to a dead father. He remembered the disgust in his mother's voice as she described Annabel's mother at the viewing at Goodin's.

"Lilymae said right out loud: 'Edward makes a fine show for a dead man. Collar starched nicely. Tie a perfect choice for the gray suit. Poseys have a style that goes with them right to the grave.' That woman has no feeling for her kin. Can you imagine a mother who would make such crass remarks in front of her children?"

Willie could. Happily, the daughter was nothing like her mother. Annabel's remarks were insightful—painfully so. He had deserved the barb the last time he appeared unannounced five years ago, on a fool's errand for the sheriff. Annabel had quoted from *The Jew of Malta*: "And besides the wench is dead."

CHAPTER THIRTY-FIVE

A RELUCTANT VISIT

N ow, Willie was on a fool's errand again. The door swung open before he knocked; Annabel stood before him, her arms crossed, her face flushed and uneasy.

"Why are you here, Willie?" Her words tumbled out defensively.

"Something a bit peculiar, Annabel. We got this complaint from Admah Reave—he's one of that odd bunch that live out in the West End." He drummed his fingers against the door jam and peered over her shoulder into an eerily silent house.

"He claims his child ran off, and his dogs trailed her scent to your property. Orville asked me to . . ." Willie stopped as though anything he might say would totally devastate this woman who had turned ashen, as she peered beyond him past the poplar break.

"Orville Bemis won't get to heaven demoralizing a good man." Her eyes were kind, but the startling statement she had just made flayed him as expertly as a medieval torturer.

She pushed past him, smelling of fruit, of fallen apricots, warm in the late summer sun.

"We need to talk, Willie. It's about those low-life Reaves. Here on the porch where we can't be heard." She paused. "Eliot and Mother are in the kitchen. And . . ." She looked fearfully past the poplars toward the main road, as though she expected an army of Reaves to charge down it at any moment.

"Everyone in this county knows that Orville Bemis scoots along, just on this side of what's legal—and sometimes crosses the line. We've known it for years, and we let him stay in office, because his fingers are in too many pots. You know that better than any of us. He needs to stay out of this."

She flushed up to the roots of her grayish blonde hair and trembled visibly, as she reached for his hand. When she had thought of Willie over the years, she remembered that one night as a romantic dream of something that was, in reality, no more than an adolescent mishap in the back of a pickup. She couldn't define what it meant. She could only desire that the memory of it remain.

Willie couldn't ignore the ruefulness in her voice, as she grasped his hand in a lover-like clutch, tentatively, and then resolutely.

She leaned into him, wrapping both of her hands around his. "You have to help me now when I need you."

At that moment, Willie could only see Annabel as she had been back then, that indestructible polyester netting blossoming about her, the 1950's version of a chastity belt that had failed her—as had he.

Annabel's words poured out in torrents: "Don't think of calling Child Protective Services. Lose her forever in that system. Flea-bitten and bruised. Semen was like glue on her legs. A child with ice-blue eyes. Eliot says they are like Mirna's. She wouldn't talk. Eliot recited they sailed away for a year and a day to the land where the bong tree grows. Then, she spoke. She laughed and said 'bong tree.' Five years. Lost for five long years in a land where . . ."

Annabel stopped with an expression of terror on her face, as though the pieces of a jigsaw puzzle that had been her family's life had begun moving around the board of their own accord and nothing would ever be within her control again. Her small plump hand nestled itself against Willie's long fingers, folding them around it like a bird's nest anchored in a cradle of tree branches.

"If I can't save her, I think I shall die." There was no trace of histrionics in Annabel's voice—just the simple, heartfelt statement of a fact.

As she watched waves of gravel spraying behind Willie's pickup that sped away between the poplars, Annabel could see her brother's shadow in the doorway and wondered what he had heard. She hadn't told him about Admah's visit early that morning.

"Which one of those Reaves do I need to go after?" The toxic shade of crimson suffusing his neck rose dangerously upward; one of his pant legs began to flap, as though a breeze had moved down the hall.

"I'm afloat, I'm afloat! When they said, No! You ain't! He was ready to faint, that unhappy old man in a boat." As bright as a tin whistle in the key of D, a small, piping voice sounded from somewhere behind Eliot, as a small hand tugged on the leg of his pants, careful to touch only the fabric.

"*He* didn't finish reading," Ave said accusingly as she moved to take Annabel's hand, careful to avoid contact with Eliot. "People's supposed to finish what they start."

Shooting Annabel a puzzled look, Eliot knelt beside Ave, careful not to touch her but so close that he appeared to be memorizing every scratch, bruise, and bugbite on her small, battered face. "If you'll go into the kitchen with your . . . with Lilymae for just a minute, I'll come back and read something even better."

He watched her taking small, measured steps down the hallway, as though she were well schooled in obedience. "As soon as I read a limerick, she moves her lips as though she's repeating it, but this is the first time she's spoken aloud—except once to Mother. Now, she's talking to you—so I can hear. She doesn't want me touching her."

He grabbed Annabel's arm, his eyes narrowing angrily. "Which Reave?"

"The one we need to stay away from until Willie comes back with a plan," Annabel said, with more confidence than she was feeling.

She picked up a boxy device from a small table in the foyer. "Willie left me his Poloroid camera. I need to take photographs of Ave without scaring her. That means getting her back into the bathtub so I can get her entire body on film."

Annabel looked hard into Eliot's hazel eyes, thinking of Ave's very blue eyes. "That's the most critical issue, Eliot. We need to prove that she is at risk if the . . . anyone tries to take her back before we can get more facts."

"Waiting for facts is a luxury I can't afford. Five long years of wondering about a child who was taken from her own life. A child raised by those barbarians. The very act of taking that child may have led to Mirna's death. I'm not done with those Reaves," Eliot raised his voice. "We'll get blood tests and that will end the legal questions."

"Willie told me that not every judge accepts blood testing to establish parental rights. He said HLA typing is considered to be 80 percent accurate, but that leaves a margin for doubt."

Her question tasted as bitter as gall, but she had to ask it. Willie had. "Considering Mirna's . . . lifestyle . . . is it possible that someone else . . ."

"Not possible!" Eliot's snarl startled her. "Mirna wasn't stupid. If a client wanted unprotected sex, Milo intervened. He wanted healthy whores."

Eliot moved against the stair banister, as though his legs would no longer support him. "We had these plans . . . to bargain with Milo . . . to get her out. Mirna said we had to choose a time when Milo was back on bennies. Then, one of her roommates guessed about her pregnancy and told him. Her friend Nadia told me that Milo had lined up an offer for the baby, and Mirna had to disappear."

Eliot sank down on the bottom step of the staircase as a small child's giggles and his mother's laughter, hoarse with disuse, drifted in unison from the kitchen. "Nadia warned me to stay away, to wait for Mirna to contact me, but I hired a clumsy detective. I botched it. Nothing strange about that. A life-long pattern for me," he muttered.

He pushed himself up and looked at Annabel out of tear-rimmed eyes, startlingly bright. "Not this time though. That's Mirna's child in there. And mine."

Pausing, with a faint flush of even more discomposure, he added: "I meant to say that she's ours, Annabel. You found her. Mirna said if she had a girl, she would call her Jelena, after her twin sister. She said Jelena's story was too hopeless for me to hear. I prefer the name you gave her. Ave rings with hope."

At that moment, the flash of morning sun slipping along the cusp of old glass in the front door lit her brother's face so sharply that Annabel saw an expression on it she had never seen before—as though desire for anything but that moment in time had been stripped away. She knew that expression. She had seen it on her father's face when he thought she and Eliot weren't looking.

No. She had not seen it; she had *felt* it. The most troubling part of childhood, Annabel thought, is that one doesn't have to *understand* what is happening to *feel* it. At that moment, Annabel's heart ached with astonishment.

As he leapt two steps at a time up the stairs, Eliot shouted down at her: "Bubblebath! Mother's bubblebath. That's the way to get her into the tub."

CHAPTER THIRTY-SIX

LOSING FACE

While Eliot slid a film pack into the deputy's Poloroid and pulled off the black cover paper, as his sister coaxed his damaged daughter into a bubblebath, Admah Reave was attempting to make sense out of what his son refused to tell as they traveled back to the Reave compound in the West End.

His wily son was not easily outfoxed. "Do you remember that fancy black car you said you found by the turnoff near the highway? About five years ago? After you boys worked on it, we sent it to Gainesville. Got a good price."

Hoser squinted into the afternoon sun and tore open a second box of powdered donuts. The wolfish expression on his face had nothing to do with cars. He was thinking about how vulnerable that big Posey house was with all the front windows, knee-high to the porch.

"Hoser, I expect you remember that car. You brought it home the morning after the miracle with Wilmy's baby in the church. I sent you to check the fence posts down by Hickory Creek. Do you recall?"

"Pontiac Firebird with a V-8 engine. I think it run over a deer or somethin'. The bumper was bad twisted. We nicked one from the salvage yard. We fixed that car up good," Hoser answered perfunctorily, his mind focused on slitting the wire screen, easing up a cranky window, and creeping through that big house until he found a terrified child. Or, she would be when he finished her punishment.

"You forgot to take the papers out of the glove compartment. I still have them. That car was registered to someone named Milo Grujic in Ft. Worth. That woman they found down by the creek was from Ft. Worth. Would you know of any connection?" Admah's voice had a puzzled tone, as though he were busily making some connections.

"I don't know nothin' about that blue-eyed woman or that man. Grandpa give us pocket money when we found cars and trucks. He was right pleased about that one." Hoser could shift a topic with the speed of a chameleon changing color.

"I think you know more about that woman than you are telling me, Hoser. How did you know she had blue eyes?"

Hoser did not modify his concentration on the powdered sugar coating his lips. Admah watched as Hoser extended a long, flickering tongue to lick the powder of donuts from his upper lip. The reptilian motion of Hoser's tongue unsettled Admah, as he was forced to acknowledge an emotion he had long forbidden.

"Heerd it some place. Forgit where."

This boy smacking his lips below his flat simian nostrils had a vague resemblance to Admah; nothing of Essie's kindness had been transmitted to a son who had siphoned the life out of his mother.

While Admah steered his truck down the washboard gravel of the road leading home, he was overcome by self-indulgent pity.

Seven half-formed boys rested along a fencerow, their names carved by Essie, with the stones weathering badly in the harsh prairie winters; only Hoser had survived, a throwback to the worst traits of the Reaves.

That miracle child of Wilmy's should have been his and Essie's. Her eyes were so translucent that he struggled to recall the exact color. A treasure of a child. A Reave would never give up a treasure.

"Find her, Hoser. Find her afore we lose face."

At midnight, the Posey's resident great horned owl surveyed several acres of adjacent fields from its post at the top of an enormous hackberry on the south side of the house. Dozens of skittering vermin tracked through the tall fronds of Big Bluestem. The "who-who, who-who" erupting from the tree paralyzed the smallest of these creatures into a momentary stasis.

The brawny specimin of vermin smashing his way through the field of native grasses heard nothing but the pounding of his own heart and saw only a dim, downstairs light in the Posey house. Rich people like the Poseys had big sleeping rooms all their own, with locking doors and mattresses stuffed with goosedown.

He stopped at the edge of the lawn and breathed in deeply. The perfume of roses, the scent of mowed grass, the great swaths of honey locust trees in bloom masked every other odor. He could no longer smell a frightened child.

Somewhere in that maze of rooms, bigger than any store in Wolfe Flats, Betty Heather hid from him. That woman who looked at him like he was dirt under her feet had probably washed the smell off Betty Heather. No matter. When he found her, she would smell of fear again.

As he tried to make himself feather light, his thick-soled boots crunched on the porch steps. He yanked at the laces and eased his feet out of the boots. He flexed two, lumpy big toes. Without years of confinement in ill-fitting boots, they might have blossomed into opposable toes.

Barefooted and cautious, Hoser skirted the windows until he reached the one with the ragged screen. He pushed his hand through the rotten wire, unlatched the screen, and lifted it away from the window.

"Who-who. Who-who." The sound of the owl startled Hoser. Under other circumstances, he'd pull the .22 out of his belt and pop that owl out of the tree. Not fit for eatin' but just for fun. All them feathers blasted to kingdom come.

The window glided up, with small chunks of putty dropping noiselessly to the floor. Hoser squeezed the top half of his body through the opening, stopped and listened, then oozed the rest of his body into the room. His tongue flickered just past his lips, primed like a snake's receptor to pick up scents.

The aroma of beeswax overpowered his senses. The waxed floors felt cool and damp under his bare feet. In the lean-to where he had lived with his Pa, Wilmy, and Betty Heather before that girl got him kicked out to the Sleep Shed, the odors were predictable: blinky milk, spoiled meat, and the faint mildew of onions and potatoes past their prime.

In the wavering light of a small lamp near the staircase, he saw gleaming wooden steps that would have taken months of hard work to get that kind of patina. The stairs led in a great, curving arc right up to what must be heaven. Pictures of cows and girls and big buildings set in what must be real gold frames led him up and up until he reached a hall that forked in two directions.

The singsong sound of a child's voice froze him. "They sailed away for a year and a day to the land where the bong tree grows." No other sounds could be heard. Just Betty Heather mouthing gibberish, the way she always did when she thought no one could hear her.

He pulled his smelly snot rag out of his back pocket. Wilmy used to wash his clothes. No one did now. With a gag in her mouth, Betty Heather wouldn't be making any noise until they reached the far end of the Posey property. Then, she could scream her head off. He'd like that. Her punishment was long overdue. If he said don't tell, she'd keep her mouth shut. Just like them little goats his pa raised to sell to the Mexicans.

If Hoser had been schooled in the arts, he would have recognized a duplicate of Munch's famous painting when he pushed open the squeaky door at the top of the stairs. Sitting upright in a large, four-poster bed, Ave clamped her hands to her ears and opened her mouth in a wide and agonizingly silent scream.

The blast of a .38 in Annabel's hand transported the painting's lovely hues of sunset red to the opposite wall.

The screamer changed positions. The one in bed crawled deeply under the covers. The one clutching a sizeable hole just beneath his left shoulder howled like a wounded beast, knocking down paintings, and Lilymae's china bibelots, as he fell and rose and fell again down the stairs and out into an indigo night.

CHAPTER THIRTY-SEVEN

CATHARSIS

The wiggle room in testing for paternity in 1981 might not prove with certainty that Ave was Eliot's daughter, but the science of HLA typing had put Eliot in the catbird seat. When the vacant-eyed Wilmy Reave, clutching her father's arm, came smiling into the Ardmore hospital laboratory to have her blood sampled, she left with a puzzled expression before the results came back, as though she knew that the ABO antigen present in Betty Heather's blood would not be found in hers.

Abner Reave preached against the testing of blood as a heathenish practice. His son Admah refused to be tested on principle, that principle being that he did not believe in miracles.

When Eliot and Annabel left Judge Overton's chambers and walked across the courthouse parking lot, she could see the social worker's car with Ave's doubtful face pressed against the window—as though the Christmas feast would always be on the other side of the glass. Annabel smiled. The imperatives of Eliot's life and her life were clearer than they might ever be again.

If the old-style serological testing had stayed in vogue, Wilmy Reave might have reclaimed Betty Heather. Annabel breathed a sigh of relief. With the isolation of the first restrictive enzyme, "reasonable doubt" for parental testing had been removed from Judge William Overton's mind.

With a mild and ruminative expession, Judge Overton appeared to be chewing over a cud of disagreeable information: a little girl found in the Posey chicken coop; an invasion of the Posey house by Hoser Reave; a trail of blood leading from Annabel Posey's bedroom down the stairs, with no Hoser to be found; and, testimony by Vernica Roberts—who had taught Judge Overton in seventh grade when he was Billy—that upended his deliberations.

"Billy, you were always a boy of two minds. For once, just make the right decision," Vernica had held up her hands, palms up, as though the scales had already been balanced.

Wearing khaki shirts like Hitler's bullyboys, the Reave men followed their leader Abner into the courthouse and lined the hall outside the courtroom. "We don't need no jailhouse lawyer to get our God-given child back to us," Abner declared to his men. "We're making a bit of a show for moral support to Admah." Only Admah, the putative father of the child, and Wilmy, who was struck dumb, when the judge asked her if she were the birth mother, represented the Reave parental interests.

A prevailing atmosphere of entitlement hovered around two Oklahoma City lawyers in bespoke suits sitting beside Eliot and Annabel Posey. Since there was no opposing counsel to inform, one of the lawyers made an official statement for the record that both of them were acquainted with the judge.

Unrehearsed witnesses testified, as the lawyers intended—openly, honestly, and sometimes clumsily, so that the judge knew that they could not have been coached. Sheriff Bemis extemporized about the alleged mother. "She was a foreign woman who refused to give my deputy complete information, so whether she brought a baby to town is pure speculation," he nodded toward Admah Reave.

Turning away from the lawyer, the sheriff addressed the judge: "I don't know how big city law works, but in Wolfe County, I have always done my dead level best to get runaway kids back to their folks. Eliot Posey took custody of Admah's little girl two weeks ago like he is above the law. Or thinks he *is* the law."

A caution from the judge didn't raise the Sheriff's hackles. Being flayed with surgical precision for dereliction of duty riled him to the point of speechlessness. The Posey lawyer ticked off so many oversights and omissions in Orville Bemis's five-year-old cold case that the Sheriff jumped to his feet and exploded: "Do you dare tar me with the brush of a murderer and a kidnapper?"

A warning by Judge Overton and a quiet "no more questions" from the lawyer sent Orville Bemis on his way and settled a part of the case that would forever remain cold.

The Reave midwife who had delivered Wilmy's baby five years earlier was nowhere to be found in the Reave compound. Deputy Helms interviewed Abner's two wives, who assisted at the birth. They described the baby as "lumpy headed and weak" before it "passed on" and attested to the fact that it came back to life in its coffin as "a miracle."

Out of Abner's earshot, one of the wives whispered to Willie: "That child looked like one of them blond angels in the Bible. She warn't. Too smart alecky by half."

Admah's refusal to submit to a blood test irked the judge. Admah's stony silence brought a contempt warning and a final crash of the gavel. Kidnapping charges hung in the judge's chambers like a noxious odor—not to be dismissed, but left, for now, as a cold case.

Judge Overton knew his county. The Reave clan had settled in Wolfe County before statehood. Their need for everything they didn't have gnawed at them. Losing a child they had claimed would whet their anger. Grim-faced Reaves stood in the hall outside his courtroom, waiting for the verdict that they knew was inevitable.

People in Wolfe County understood the meaning of dominion. The line segmenting caste might look invisible, but it was deeply etched. The obligation to do battle shored up both sides of that line. Messages that instill fear can mildew in the legal system and yet do mischief.

Honor for everyone might be better served by keeping the kidnapping charge in the chiller. The threat of it might stay there forever, unless the Poseys took the high road. Judge Overton shrugged off his robe and thought about the scales of justice. How they sometimes balanced perfectly, in spite of human manipulation.

With the weight of evidence of malfeasance falling around him like lost votes in the upcoming election, Orville Bemis finally ventured into the West End on official business and found Admah pouring buckets of rancid peanuts into the hog troughs.

"Hate to press you when you've just had all this trouble, Admah, but do you know the whereabouts of Hoser?'

Admah stared at the sheriff's neck, as though fascinated by the two pendulous dewlaps on the ears nestled just above a bolo with a gumdrop-sized turquoise stone.

The afternoon sun reflected an odd glint in Admah's eyes that might have been subdued fury or simply inexpressible fatigue. "Questions too large to answer shouldn't be asked."

Just before the sun dropped off the edge of the prairie, Annabel sat by her mother on the porch swing, their quartet of heels companionably controlling the ebb and flow of the swing. They smiled at a shrieking urchin, clutching the mane of a fat dappled pony that was doing serious damage to Lilymae's garden of roses.

Holding a long lead while chanting, "knees in, back straight" with the solemnity and rapt expression of a pleased choirmaster, Eliot watched Ave bobbing among the roses.

Annabel recognized that look; an image of their father darted into her memory, the way the sun torches the prairie for an instant and drops off the edge of the world, as though such brightness had never been.

Eliot was observing Ave with that same intenseness that Annabel recalled on her father's face when he didn't think anyone was looking. It was an expression that offers everything and desires nothing, as though all the trappings of love have been transcended.

Annabel glanced at her mother, who was squashing herself uncomfortably close, her small prunish mouth making soft noises at the pony in her rose garden, urging it on, breathing in deeply, as though the crushed rose petals acted as an elixir.

Just beyond the bend of poplars, Willie Helms' pickup popped into view. On one arm, waving nonchalantly out the window, Annabel could see the faded blue of a denim work shirt. Willie wasn't coming to visit as a deputy. It might even be a different Willie, one whose life wasn't derailed by ice on Highway 77.

For a single, splendid moment, Annabel could see the patterns, the way that lives intersected, as though somewhere in the universe a lever has been pressed and the world is sorted again. She knew that if we live it in the best way, the right way, all life is sacrifical.

She said softly—and to no one in particular––"Until then, like Hephzibah always said: 'We make do.'"

The End

NOVELS BY PEGGY GARDNER

A Winding Sheet

The Land Trilogy

   Land of the Bong Tree

   Land of Nod

   Land of Lyonesse

Clio at War

Clio in the Crossfire

Made in the USA
Monee, IL
15 January 2021

57664350R00144